CONFESSIONS OF QUIET WINNERS

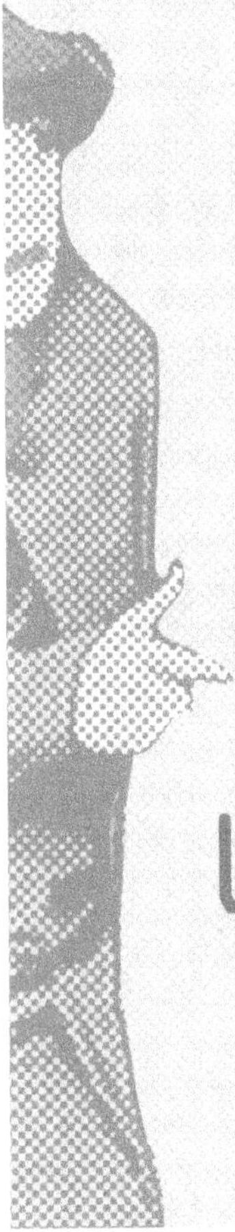

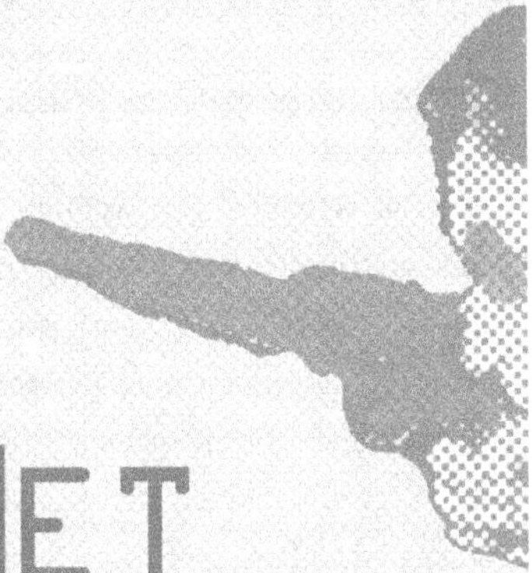

<ryan e. long>

CONTENTS

PREFACE

In today's fast food paced media cycle, many untrue facts are either intentionally or negligently reported as true. This isn't new. Truth, like a grass fed pig covered in mud, has been evading our grasping hands for centuries.

Even with tech advancements like artificial intelligence ("AI"), some false – or "fake" -- news is never exposed. That's because humans need to properly program AI with accurate information. AI can't flag a counterfeit Mona Lisa without knowing what the original looks like. Wrong inputs lead to wrong outputs. Some of these outputs are obviously wrong, such as -- "AI: Mona Lisa is blond." This would be obvious to someone familiar with the original. Even when AI is fed the right data set, it can misidentify a painting as a Mona Lisa when it's not. And so AI algorithms can be good at counting the number of counterfeit Mona Lisa paintings in a location. But they can't tell you what that stockpile means.

That's why human intelligence is even more important as sophisticated technologies proliferate. This is especially true when an insider has information concerning, say, the counterfeit Mona Lisa.

Before you know it, the next news cycle starts. We can unknowingly accept yesterday's untruth as truth today. As new fake news builds upon old fake news, the damage caused by the original puny fake news gets multiplied as time "progresses." What is more, it becomes harder to detect the original error because of all the additional layers of fake news camouflaging it.

The reputable and not so reputable characters in this novella have fun stealthily gaining intelligence. To find out more about their family histories, please read my other books. In the meantime, get thrilled and chuckle reading the following pages.

Ryan E. Long

/Chapter 1:

=TIJUANA MISSILE _CRISIS

The terror warning suddenly arrives on my cell phone from *The New York Times*:

XXX DIRTY BOMB SCARE
NEW YORK CITY'S GRAND CENTRAL TERMINAL

Today is Tuesday, October 17, 2017, about 10:00 a.m.

I think this was the 78th bomb scare this year. I'm 48 years old, and thought I'd seen it all. Evidently, I have not.

I sit in the middle of the coffee break room at the Veterans Affairs hospital in Brooklyn, where I am this Walt Whitman looking bearded psychiatrist. I look away from my cell phone to the front page of *The New York Times* in my hand. The headline reads:

TURKEY BOMBED BY RED-COLORED STEALTH
FIGHTER JETS
RUSSIANS SUSPECTED
MASSIVE CASUALTIES TOTALLY REPORTED

"Shit," I say to myself, "it's time for agent Wilson's dinner pill." I put down the newspaper and walk over to his room. When I get there, I see this Nordic looking volleyball player tall nurse, one who'd drop me before the first round, walk out of his room and smile at me.

"Good evening, Doctor Egan," the nurse says.

"Good evening, Nurse Isaacs," I say back to her, staring at her nametag, as she hands me her report on agent

Skip Wilson. I've never seen this nurse before, and figure she is new.

I head into agent Wilson's hospital room, and ask him:

"Are you ready for your next pill?"

Wilson doesn't bother looking up, but just keeps reading today's *Washington Post*. I take the paper out of his hands.

"Already?" He asks, staring at me through his dodgy black Ray-Ban sunglasses, which maybe explain why his main spy name is "Dodgy Bond," a sort of raffish *Beach Boy* version of James Bond.

"It's time," I look at my Casio watch.

My name is Dr. Liam Egan, and I'm a fancy Harvard trained psychiatrist from the South Side of Chicago. Skip Wilson is a veteran Central Intelligence Agency ("CIA") agent who I have been treating now for a few months due to his nervous breakdown, which, according to his superiors who put him here, happened when he was serving in Kiev, Ukraine. Behind closed doors, they want him deemed "sane" so that he can stand trial for treason.

"Alright," Wilson finally takes the pill in his hand, and appears to drink it with the water. He then zips up his black Fila tracksuit top and appears to go to sleep.

"I'll be back Thursday morning for our appointment," I say as I walk out.

"Yeah, yeah," Wilson says as he crosses his arms, "bring me a croissant while you at it and an Americano, no sugar."

I ignore him.

After I exit Skip's room, I go back to drink my coffee in the break room and open up my computer. That's when I read another headline in my e-mail, this from *The Wall Street Journal*:

HOT RUSSIAN HOT RODS
SPOTTED IN TIJUANA!

According to the *Journal* article that I open, "large black hard hot rods were seen in Tijuana by artificial intelligence in a satellite doing recon in Mexicoa." A link to an article in MIT Technology Review about bad AI technology and some of the misidentification errors – along with causes – is on the right side of the screen.

The text of the journal article explains the relevance of the rods: "these are the same types of hot rods used for plutonium manufacturing in Russian missiles." Weird, cause when I look at the photo, the black timber looking rods look like the same ones I'd seen in civilian aerospace manufacturing, part of Tijuana's industry.

I peer up at the ceiling in the hospital.

I think about the proof of Weapons of Massive Distraction ("WMD") found in the country of Crack, years before, under President Gin Rush's administration. I remember an old blind grandmother in the city of Baggy, Crack, whose account of the WMD was recorded. I look up her account online on my laptop, and find this translation from Arabic:

> *Ooh, I think I smelled the weapon! It was steaming all around me, smelling like sulfur, maybe even rotten eggs. That's when I knew it had to be bulging, kind of like how the Hulk's muscles just go all over the place, but exceedingly tidier than that, you know?*

But then I remember, in the recording that was unedited, another voice, this of an old grandpa, also speaking in Arabic. His translated recording was right next to hers:

> *Give me a break, woman. You could put a*

*Mexican bean-eating champ under the table with
your smelly weapon.*

Based on such intelligence, in addition to photos from
a satellite similar to the ones that this man eating a Subway
sandwich took of the Tijuana hot rods, President Rush ordered
an invasion of Crack. This is so even though President Gin
Rush's father, President Herb Rush, would have not ousted
Crack's dictator, President Sandy Hussy, at least according
to *A Galaxy Transformed*, President Herb Rush's memoir.

Suddenly, my phone rings when I get another e-mail.
I look down and see it's another message in my in box from
The Wall Street Journal, with the following heading:

*TIJUANA MISSILE CRISIS
RESIDENTS GETTING
"SO, LIKE TOTALLY READY, MAN"*

Opening up the e-mail, I see a photo of a mustached
taco-cart "entrepreneur," name Mario Sanchez, who told the
Journal:

*If these gringos come busting my cart, I demand
like all arbitration clauses in my contracts be all
null and void, cause this all act of God, or, actually, act of stupid gringos, type of things. So if
we going down this road, all because some Russian hackers be putting missiles in burritos down
here, it not my fault, and I demand, what they call
it, a bond for my damages from gringo missiles.*

When asked about whether he was worried about his
safety, Mr. Sanchez said, "no way, cause I got like a bunker
in Washington D.C., where they be like a hurricane party
when all this goes down."

Scrolling down further, another Tijuana local, Fernando
Sanchez, says:

Yeah, but what they going to do when all of them hot GM, Ford, and Toyota models in New York and bankers at Golding Sacks don't get their nose candy? Don't be knocking on my door, complaining to me, cause I get my job done, clean like a shave. Make my words . . .

The interviewer interrupted, you mean "mark your words?"

Mark them if you want, whatever, but just be all taking note that I got like all important gringo clients in New York, Vegas, Holly Weed, and they not going be not happy if they wake up one morning, and they don't have my Einstein Bag® of tricks and treats next to their bed, ready to be eaten, at the end of their Halloween day, or before it.

Truth is, this whole Tijuana missile crisis makes me sick to my stomach. So I get up, pack up, and I travel back home to my relaxing cabin in Oyster Bay, Long Island, a shack that's been passed down for generations. But I still couldn't keep my curiosity at bay of answering this question: how did this Tijuana missile crisis happen? So I open my laptop computer in my home office, and open up agent Wilson's voluminous CIA file, which includes his e-mails over the years, diary entries, and even some video recordings. I start reading. I discover the dominos leading to the crisis apparently started falling in and around the time Skip arrived in Kiev a few years ago on February 14, 2014.

The following e-mail shows why.

/Chapter 2:

+VODKA...JALAPENO

Dude, can't wait until we get back to Tijuana! It's colder than a witch's tit here in Kiev.

So reads this e-mail from agent Wilson to one Sasha Stravinska on February 15, 2014, the day after Wilson arrived in Kiev. According to Wilson's file, him and this Sasha were boyhood friends from Brighton Beach, Brooklyn. The e-mail string continues, this time from Stravinska to Wilson.

No way dude, witches have hot tits. Anyway, I guess we won't be able to get back to Tijuana until what, like 2017, or something? Bummer!

The e-mails, alone, would have been harmless.
But Sasha is no regular Brooklyn native.
According to Wilson's file, at the time the e-mails were exchanged, Sasha, who has aliases like "Vodka Jalapeno," was "this totally handsome (for sure a model on the side) all-star agent of the Great Red Underwear, or G-R-U, Russia's version of the CIA."
A little more than a month after the largest leak of CIA's hacking technologies in history, on March 7 of this year, agent Wilson was forcibly admitted to this hospital. According to this e-mail I received from CIA Director Stan Still shortly after Wilson's Easter admission:

They were obviously planning something nefarious, un-American, which would had been easy to do cause this Wilson was but a useful idiot for this Russian commie bastard. It is no coincidence that CIA just had the biggest leak ever. Do you dig what the hell is going on here, doctor? A perversion of our security all because this Russian has raped Wilson's mind, used their childhood friendship from Brooklyn as a way to crowbar his way into Wilson's soul, his spirit, his psyche, and, who knows, maybe his ass? Get him deemed sane, so we can try his ass for treason. Wilson's the one who leaked our files.

Of course, there is a lot more evidence to support the charges that Wilson was a "useful idiot" for his Russian friend Sasha, including Wilson's diary entries. But e-mails like the one above between the Brighton boys "were just the tip of the commie iceberg," according to Director Still. I flip through some more e-mails on my laptop, sipping a green tea in my home office, and find this one between the two Brighton Boys, using their nicknames – "Dodgy Bond" for agent Wilson, "Vodka Jalapeno" for agent Stravinska:

From: Dodgy Bond
To: Vodka Jalapeno
Re: Tijuana
Date: February 15, 2014

Can't wait to play our dirty tricks on those kinky American chicks once we get back to Tijuana. You know how it's going to go.

From: Vodka Jalapeno
To: Dodgy Bond
Re: Tijuana
Date: February 15, 2014

Hot! You know they are going to love it.

7

They won't be able to get us out of the history books.

I peek back at the CIA analyst's report in Wilson's file. It reads:

Obviously, these e-mails show, with a high degree of reasonable, rational, and circular reasoning, that the Russians were using this Wilson as their useful idiot, and have been planning for years on putting those missiles in Tijuana.

Wondering if Wilson's diary entries would really make things worse, I flip to them before I go to bed. I open up this one, dated February 16, 2014, and I shake my head:

Man, going out with Ilia tonight to some "hot night club," in his words, outside of Kiev, but exchanging these e-mails with Sash yesterday got me thinking about Tijuana. People are going to flip the fuck out when I head back there. I think chicks are going to be shaking in their boots, especially ones who live close to the border, when they see me and Sasha walking around, back on the circuit, cause this time they'll see our manly missiles are like so ready to burst all over them.

In still another diary entry that I have here on my laptop, and which I peer at, Skip remembers back to his feelings of inferiority when he was young, and how having these "manly missiles" will get him and Sasha more respect:

Those assholes outside Tijuana didn't respect me and Sash before, looking down on us, calling us "twats" and "good for nothing dorks." Even those filthy rich women inside sometimes made fun of us, pinching our cheeks like we were just little children to be played with, not to be respected, like the men we were.

It doesn't matter. Cause Sash and I are going to go back there, to Tijuana, with those manly missiles we grew and fostered for so many years, and these women from the border will be on their knees, mouths open, waiting for us to give it to them, the biggest explosions they have ever seen, ones their nice little boxed in worlds along the border won't give to them. Ooh, can't wait for that T-Day, kind of like D-Day, but only in Tijuana.

Hoping that there may be something in Wilson's other e-mails to Sasha on February 15, 2014 that would help his case, I get discouraged when I read this string of e-mails:

From: Dodgy Bond
To: Vodka Jalapeno
Re: Tijuana
Date: February 15, 2014

Dude, so can't wait to get those women wet with our secret missiles, especially those stuck up ones from California, do you remember them when we used to hit up Tijuana when we were younger? When they see what we've been working on, they are going to be falling over themselves to get on their knees when they see our rad hot rods -- especially mine, needless to say.

According to the flight records from United Airlines in Wilson's CIA file, it appears that the two boys' families had in fact traveled to Tijuana for vacation, or at least flew into the airport on previous occasions when they were younger. I peek at another e-mail between them that day:

From: Vodka Jalapeno
To: Dodgy Bond
Re: Tijuana
Date: February 15, 2014

Da, the pussy with the military man is going to be wanting more of me, but you for the seconds, cause I the taller and have the more experience, you remember this times I having with that one in Tijuana? Is the very funny. I not think they going to be expecting these missiles we having, cause I remembering when they look at mine, say the thing like "oh little boy got the very small missile, going to write a crayon story for me?"

This was the very embarrassed, even though is the night that ending on the good note, remembering this bullshit bleached women with their attitudes cause they go to the pretty schools, thinking this making them the pretty women? They going to love it when they have my Ivan the Irritable missile there, cause you know this is what they needing, not the kissy bank boy they ordering around, this American puritan that does not see what we see, da?

Turning the page on my computer, I checked out another e-mail between the two agents, this one copied to one "Bill Bakes":

From: Dodgy Bond
To: Jalapeno Vodka
CC: Bill Bakes
Re: Tijuana
Date: February 15, 2014

Dude, your written English has gotten

fresh off the yacht sounding – take some brush up English courses. Anyway, so, all I know is that we won't have to worry about any more attacks, cause, as I understand the Me So Boring technology, they won't want to come around us anymore when we are with the women in Tijuana. I mean, before when we went to Tijuana, they always threatened us with their bigger missiles, always totally making us not in the mood to have any good times. But the Me So Boring is so cool! I can't believe we'll be able to finally have fun in Tijuana without worrying about being bullied all because of our puny hot rods, cause the Me So Boring technology will make up for it.

> *From: Vodka Jalapeno*
> *To: Dodgy Bond*
> *CC: Bill Bakes*
> *Re: Tijuana*
> *Date: February 15, 2014*

Da, da, my written English is getting super shitty, but who cares? What are we, in Dead Poet's Society? Anyway, is the very funny, this Me So Boring software. I not believe nothing when we make this, is the very, how you say, guard of the front? Nyet, avant garde is what I mean. When I seeing it, all I could think about is when they seeing us, they not going to be thinking we the easy prey no more, cause Me So Boring going to make Me So Horney in the Tijuana, nyet? Da, da, is the rhetoric question, is how you say.

When I flip back to Wilson's diary entries, I find that they confirm CIA Director Still's suspicion that he thought of this *Me So Boring* technology as something they would use to "make their big massive hot rod" work all the better, according to Wilson's following entry:

> *Oh man, so stoked about this software me and Sash wrote, going to be like totally cool when they check it in Tijuana, cause those chicks were all like doubting us before but now they'll be all like drooling all over our grown up missile silos when we go back there. They'll finally take Sash and I seriously for once, with their big cars, hair, nails, bank accounts, especially those loaded border women.*

> *They would always be all pinching us in our cheeks, thinking we were too small and too young to make them happy. Whatever! They are going to see how wrong they are when they see how the software works when we get back to Tijuana. They'll will be leaving their older sugar daddies for us, wanting to pay me and Sash our properly fair free market value, not this crony capitalist bullshit, cause they'll know more why quiet winners do it best.*

Reading the diary entries, and e-mails, makes me sort of depressed. I feel like it is going to be an open and shut case against Wilson, and that insanity would not likely be a defense given his obvious ability to engage in means-end reasoning. Sick of reading this stuff, I close my laptop and go to sleep.

Two days later, on Thursday, October 19, 2017, it's about 10:00 a.m. and I am about to go and see Wilson in his room for our second session during this Tijuana missile crisis. Then, weird, I get this bizarre text from Director Stan Still:

From: Stan Still
To: Dr. Liam Egan
Re: Agent Wilson
Date: October 19, 2017

Doctor, I know you are just trying to do your job, but we are getting antsy, not in a kid waking up on Christmas morning fun (!) type of antsy, about this agent Wilson. Dig me? We need some confirmation of his sanity—now--so that we can get him in prison sooner rather than later. I mean, come on doctor, it's not going to do any good when they world is blown up, right? Don't need to go to Harvard Medical School to figure this one out. Thanks for hurrying it up, and doing your duty to your country.

Sincerely,
SS

How could I carry out my ethical duty and properly evaluate this patient, in an unbiased way, when Director Still was breathing down my neck for the answer he wanted? I thought to myself: Isn't such tell you what you want to hear, not what you need to hear, intelligence what got us into that war in Crack and ousted Sandy Hussy?

Walking through the hospital hallway to Wilson's room, I come across a brunette nurse, country French looking, with freckles and slightly pink lipstick, who smiles at me. I wonder to myself when I'll get a date with a woman like her.

Must have been a new nurse, or one transferred in from somewhere else, cause I don't think I'd seen her before. I shrugged, not thinking anything of it, cause the Brooklyn VA hospital is massive, and there is big time turn over of nurse personnel.

I walk into Wilson's room and he is wide-awake, sitting reading a *Carnegie Mellon Today* magazine through his sunglasses. I think I smell perfume in the air.

"What ye reading?" I ask.

"*Cosmopolitan*," he says as he puts down the *Carnegie Mellon Today* magazine blowing what looked like a little smoke from his mouth.

"Smell something?" I ask as I look around.

"Smell what?" He sniffs his hand.

"Smells like perfume in here," I say.

Wilson reaches over to the metal nightstand. He pulls out some fine looking cologne bottle and sprays it right next to this black birthmark on the right side of his neck.

"Smell better now?" He asks.

"Now it smells like an expensive skunk," I say.

"No doubt he's expensive," Wilson massages his whiskered face, a beard that wasn't *Gentleman's Quarterly* stubble, but wasn't Moses, either.

I smirk and take a seat next to his bed. I review his faint heartbeat and such. All look pretty abnormal to me, which is why he is in here. I open up my laptop to start asking him some questions about his e-mails and diary entries again, as I think the effects, or causes, of his too smart for his own good outlier way of thinking will be found in them.

"Want some?" He holds up a bottle of Perrier to me.

"No thanks, I have my own," I point to the thermos of water in my messenger bag. As he gargles the fancy water, I start with my questions.

"So you do know, don't you, that Director Still thinks you and your friend Sasha were responsible for putting these missiles in Tijuana?"

He shrugs.

He picks up the magazine back up.

"I didn't know that," he finally says, "cause to me those missiles look like industrial chocolate used in making fancy chocolate." He flips the page of the magazine. "Or maybe even some stuff they use in Tijuana civilian aerospace manufacturing." He flips another page. "But they aren't missiles." He looks up and stares at me. He then looks back towards his mag.

"Even though the AI in our satellites has said, with high confidence, that those are rods used to create missiles in Tijuana?"

He flips the pages of the magazine, shrugging again, as he says:

"I read once in a *Rob Report* how Skinny Carlo, the Mexican billionaire, has these extravagant parties, where pools of chocolate await to be swam in, and he often gets all of his chocolate custom made in Switzerland, wholesale shipments delivered by, what's that's company called," he looks up to the ceiling, "yeah, real funny name, like Einstein Trucking."

He looks over at me.

He then says, "or maybe those rods are used to make airplane skeletons in that factory down there. Airplane wings like long rods in them, too, you know," he smiles then turns his attention back to the magazine.

"Let's get serious, agent Wilson," I say sort of stern, lassoing him back in.

He peers back at me through his sunglasses, which he has refused on numerous occasions to take off on threat of doing "unexpected damage."

"Alright, doc, I didn't know that Still thinks me and Sash put the 'missiles' there," he drops the magazine on the top of his bed sheet to put quotation marks around the word "missiles."

"How could you not?" I ask.

He puts out his hand and rests it on my knee, his black Fila track suit top hugging his speed bump belly, long hair dangling on his shoulders.

"I'm fucking with you, doc," he says, then pulls his hand off my knee.

"So you know why Director Still suspects you of treason?"

"Yeah, because he never grew up as a younger perverted oddball boy in Brooklyn like I did."

"Come again?"

"Me and Sash were filthy minded boys growing up in Brighton," he says, "and anything we say about Tijuana in those e-mails has nothing to do with the Mexican city."

"How so?" I ask.

He nods to my lap top.

"*Tijuana* was a joint in Brighton Beach me and Sash used to go to as teens," he then says.

I open up my Google Platinum on my laptop and look for the club on the Internet.

"You aren't going to find it, doc. It was an underground club."

"Underground meaning illegal?"

He stacks the *Carnegie Mellon Today* magazine on top of the other reading materials next to his bed, and picks up an edition of *Forbes*.

"I'd prefer to say underground means VIP, and that they didn't want to have to be all complying with anti-discrimination, equal opportunity, controlled substances, and all of the other laws which make fun into the new 'f' word."

"Whose they?" I ask. I open my Moleskin to take notes.

"Those cats who ran the club when I was younger."

"What type of place was this?" My pen is ready to write.

He turned the page of *Forbes* magazine and calmly shrugged while he said:

"A little nail salon mixed in with some with fresh Baja style Mexican cafe mixed in with a cozy nightclub mixed with private dating booths mixed with some private equity and wicked Blue Bottle coffee."

I write down in my notebook:

"*Tijuana* – patient says it was a Dragon's den in Brooklyn."

"What about all of these references to hot rods in your e-mails and diary entries?"

"Oh, yeah," he peaks over to my computer, "Sash and I always used code words for things, cause we knew that our e-mails were never secure, always could be peered at by the prying eye, and so we used 'hot rods' to mean our little peckers, or at least mine."

I look down to my notebook:

"Hot rods – patient says means their peckers, patient's was 'puny' at the time."

Looking back to Wilson, I ask:

"Alright, so, yeah, you and Sasha went to this underground lair as kids, but how old were you guys?"

"We used to go from the time we were about 13 until we graduated Brooklyn Tech."

"And these kinds of people who ran this supposed club let you kids in even though you were under age?"

"Yeah, we washed the dishes in the start, did all of their crap work, getting rid of mice with our cats, washing the customers' clothes in the mornings, you name it, we did it."

Wilson flashes the article he is reading, *Encryption Technology Goes To XXX Valley*, to me as if it were a centerfold. I wave it away, and he goes back to reading it.

"And how did you get these jobs, I mean, how did you know they were hiring?"

He jots a note down onto the article he is reading with his pencil as he says:

"My pop knew one of the owners, got me and Sash hooked up with the jobs. My mom always thought I was working at Sasha's pop's coffee house."

I rub my beard, wondering if Wilson was a savant liar, or telling me the truth.

"And what about this *Me So Boring* technology?"

"Oh, yeah, that," he jots something else down, "it's a software algorithm that uses your own technology's strength against you."

"Did you know that Director Still says this technology that you and Sasha created is used in those Russian missiles in Tijuana so that you'd finally not feel like the 'thug meat heads' you are, in his words?"

I look down at one of Director Still's e-mails to make sure I got it right.

Wilson waves me off.

"Yeah, well, I don't need to read what Still has said about me, cause he always painted me with the outlier weirdo who couldn't be trusted brush."

"So you are saying this *Me So Boring* technology can't be used for offensive purposes, only defensive ones?"

"Offensive, defensive, whatever label you want to put on it. It was written to stop maniacs who think they will survive a nuclear holocaust from starting one, from sitting in their bunkers or wherever they are and thinking that they will make it out fine, while others sit and sniff unhealthy radioactive coke."

I write down in my diary: "*Me So Boring* – Wilson's dangerous druggie fantasy?"

"And you thought that the women at *Tijuana* would think differently of you once they saw what you and Sasha had written this code, all grown up and all?"

"Wouldn't you want to buy someone lunch who you believed could prevent World War III from happening with their technology?"

"I suppose it depends how big the dick is," I say with a wry Irish smirk.

Wilson laughs.

"Not very big," he looks down, "but bigger than it used to be when Sash and I used to go to *Tijuana*."

"So you guys were oddballs at the club?"

"Well, hello, yeah, I mean we were the only juniors there. All of the customers used to pinch our cheeks, even though me and Sash wanted to be taken seriously like the customers."

I started reviewing some of the e-mails between Sasha and Skip.

"What about this talk about the 'border' I see in this e-mail. Director Still says how this shows you were talking about the Mexican-U.S. border, and how you wanted to intimidate people, especially women, along there."

Wilson opens up the *Forbes* magazine to stare at a centerfold, I presume to be of some complicated financial strategy, and says over to me:

"Not surprised Director Still wants to make me look like Ted Kaczynski, some wild-eyed terrorist, but the fact is me and Sash was talking about the Brooklyn and Queens border."

"Okay, so you have this club, you have this border, you have this software, but it still doesn't explain who this Bill Bakes is that you copied on these e-mails."

"Yah, doc, it doesn't."

Wilson picks at a piece of sushi that was left on his nightstand with some wooden chopsticks. He holds out what looked like a California roll for me to take.

"Want one?"

I look behind me. The door is closed.

"Why not?"

I take the California roll into my mouth, and start to enjoy it more with each chew, when I get another buzz kill alert on my iPhone, this one from *The Washington Post*:

PRESIDENT NOELL HESS CHANGES
TERROR LEVEL TO BLOODY MARY ORANGE

I look up and watch Wilson calmly eating his sushi, reading his *Forbes*, and wonder why he wasn't worrying about any of this craziness. Up to that time, he hadn't expressed outrage, fear, or even sadness about the Tijuana missile crisis.

Suddenly, he flashes an article to me in *Forbes*, titled *"Off The Grid Wealth,"* about Queen Elizabeth II of England, which lists her as the richest person in the world. He smirks then puts the magazine on the nightstand as the alarm on my computer goes off, indicating the session is over.

"See you next time, doc," he says nonchalantly, putting more sushi in his mouth. "Want one for the road?"

I slowly get up, "no thanks, but see you next time, Wilson."

I leave the room and head to my next appointment.

On my way home to Oyster Bay later that night, I wonder to myself: maybe Wilson wasn't the "schizophrenic traitor" that Director Rummage and some others of the CIA made him out to be?

I'd find out more during my third session with Wilson during the missile crisis.

/CHAPTER 3:

<BRIGHTON HACKING BEACH/

"We always wondered if Bernice Brownstone was an international Mob boss," Wilson suddenly says. It is Tuesday, October 24, 2017, about 10:00 in the morning.

Wilson rarely opened up, so I didn't want to miss this opportunity.

"Why was that?" I ask him, Moleskin on my lap.

He looks at me through his shades.

"Cause Sash and I would always see her during those summers in Brighton swimming in the ocean, cigarette in her mouth, doing a crappy breaststroke, wearing a torn and frayed swim cap, saggy bathing suit with her tit almost hanging out, after she'd have her meetings here and there with men wearing suits or tracksuits or both."

I play along with him, as this can often get the most of out patients.

"An unglamorous winner she was?" I asked.

"You could say that. So Director Still wouldn't take her seriously."

Like a parrot not knowing what he is saying, I nod in agreement.

He picks back up the *Forbes Magazine* he was reading during our previous session and flips it back to the *Off The Grid Wealth* article. As he does, I peer at his diary entry below about this Brighton Beach granny. I have a feeling she had a lot to do with agent Wilson's treatment, or what Director Still called "investigation," for "outlier thoughts unbecoming of a trustworthy CIA officer."

She would always be there in the mornings when we went to school, sipping coffee with a bunch of her friends, but they wasn't women, see. All of these men in mostly track suits would be sitting around her, all with gray hair, and they'd be smoking cigarettes, going over papers, and me and Sash always wondered if she was a high end madam, smoking so many cigarettes that she'd make a New York City cockroach look like a health nut from Northern California.

Used to think she was just a boring retiree maybe, from the city, until one day I see this man who used to be with her in the mornings, massive mammoth man, biggest arms you'd ever see, on the front page of the New York Post, cause he was found fully clothed and dead as a rat in the East River. The Post said it was a suicide, and even had some statements from his friends saying how he was depressed and all, but I thought different that one-day when Bernice Brownstone showed me those eyes.

She usually wore these massive black-framed sunglasses with aqua blue tinted lenses, I mean they'd cover her whole eye sockets. But one morning me and Sash was talking and walking on the boardwalk, heading to school, when I looked over, and through her cigarette smoke, through all of the papers on the table, I saw a peek of her snake green eyes, like you'd see on a Frankenstein, so scary next to her paper white German-Russian skin. Remember her looking at me while she cleaned her black sunglasses, and she had a murderous glance to her eyes.

*It was then and there I knew she was what
Sash and I liked to call a "quiet winner."*

After reading his entry, I look up at Wilson. He says as he reads:

"Yeah, yeah, Director Still would have thought Brownstone was some has been loser who'd never amount to anything in her life, no degree from Princeton or anything like that."

"Cause Still's a Princeton man, and Brownstone probably dropped out of high school?" I asked.

Wilson zips down his black Fila tracksuit top and puts his *Forbes* magazine on top of the stack of other reading materials on his nightstand. He picks up another *Carnegie Mellon Today* magazine, starts flipping through it, then says:

"Yeah, school would have been too expensive of a proposition."

"High opportunity cost?" I ask, tapping my pen.

"Yea, that," he nods as he holds open the magazine to show me the centerfold for the month of October 2017. "Now who needs Prozac if you can look at computer code like that?"

"Good question," I nod, "maybe we should write and ask the code?"

Wilson and I chuckle.

"So I gather that you and Sasha had a fascination with Brownstone while growing up in Brighton?"

"You could say that, I mean, it was in old New York. Everyone didn't always flash their money around, showing you how much they had and where they were going with it."

He flips the page in the magazine.

"How do you mean?" I ask.

"You know when cats were in high school, and they would brag about their first time?"

"Yeah, I suppose so, it's a big part of growing up," I say, wondering where he is heading.

"Well, me and Sash had our first time, and we didn't tell a soul, cause that was the way things were done in New York City at the time."

"Why?"

"Cause of where it all happened."

"Where did it all happen, your first time, in a North Korean brothel?"

He giggles.

"It was more locked down than a North Korean brothel."

"And where was that?"

"*Tijuana*."

He puts the magazine down, slowly gets up.

"I got to drop the kids off, doc, be back in a little."

He picks up copies of the recent Brazilian and French *Vogue* magazines that were on the lower level of his nightstand, and walks over to the bathroom. As I listen to him singing his awful rendition of *Midnight Rider* in the bathroom, I peek down at my laptop to this diary entry about his "first time" at *Tijuana*:

> Me and Sash was washing dishes one night, in the back, when Mario the manager came in and asked us to "like, get all freshened up, pronto," he said as he directed us to down to the bathroom. We walked down the candle lit steps to the black tiled bathroom in the basement, and Willie Robinson, the caretaker, also known as "Brownie," greeted us.
>
> "Boys, this is your special night," the tuxedoed mocha skinned surrogate grand pop with the perfect manicure said to us.

"What, I am getting the Michael Jackson glove to wash the dishes?" Sash asked.

"Better," Brownie said, his slim mustache hugging his upper lip, as he directed us to go into the bathroom stall. When me a Sash went into the stall, there were two custom tuxedos for us to wear, shoes and all. We got dressed, walked out, and Brownie got off the phone.

"You cats are going to have some times tonight," he said after he took out his earpiece and directed us over to his Asprey cologne tray. "Sprinkle some on your ears, and then come with me."

We was just 18 at the time, I remember cause it was right before Sash and I got our acceptance letters to go to college.

When we got out into the main dining room, there was a lit up puny taco truck going through the tables making martinis, tacos, and a little, what they call it, seafood appetizers. I remember Sash and I looking at each other as some of the prettiest women we'd ever seen was waving us over to their booth.

Of course, we didn't want to be obnoxious, so we did a little pinky high five down below where none of the adults could see. I could tell Sash was nervous, cause his pinky was shaking. Hell, mine was too!

So Sash and I walked over to the booth of four women, some was married, cause we could see rings on some of their hands. But what hap-

pened in Tijuana stayed in Tijuana. So we go and sit with these broads, some looking social-ite, others look model and stuff, and they played with our ties, caressed our cheeks, and poured us champagne.

A tall-married blond was sitting next to me. She had the prettiest tits I had ever seen, cause they only tits I had seen before that were the Rai-sin Bran ones of one of the grannies who used to swim topless at Brighton. I remember that night cause I couldn't keep my eyes off of the blonde's tits, which I think made her feel good, maybe cause her husband didn't appreciate her like an 18 year old Brighton boy who jerked off almost every day did.

Looked over and I see Sash with this mo-cha skilled model looking broad, and there was a read headed hot soccer mom from Connecticut on his other side. He smiled devilishly at me as the red head had her hand below, massaging him I think, with the mocha chick all kissing on his neck.

This blonde broad next to me got my at-tention when she started playing with my small excuse for a pecker, the one Sash used to call "melted turtle wax." Meanwhile, another Euro looking brunette kissed my neck, worried I was going to cream in my pants before we got to the main course. As I nervously sat between the most beautiful women I'd seen live, I nervously peeked over, and there she was:

Bernice Brownstone!

Sitting in a black blouse with the same men she'd be sitting next to when I'd see her in the mornings, she lifted her martini glass to me. I could tell she didn't have those killer eyes behind those black oversized glasses, cause she smirked through her hot hit pink lipstick.

My eyebrows went through my forehead!

Who needs Santa Claus when you got Brownstone?

Who would have known? I wondered at the time if she was the owner of Tijuana? But I didn't wonder long cause, before I knew it, the two women who towered over me took me to the back room, where I spent the night. I'll never forget the next morning, when I saw Sash get out of the room next to mine, him saying in his deadpan while shrugging:

"Every other time is going to be fucking retirement Jew in South Beach epic, eh?"

Suddenly, I hear Wilson flush the toilet, light a match, and open the door.

"Like my diaries, doc?" He says as he sits down and picks the magazine back up.

"Well, um," I uncross my legs and cross them in the other direction, "I was reading about your first time."

He smirks.

"So you read about Brownstone sitting there?"

"And yet Director Still wouldn't have thought twice about dismissing Brownstone as a quiet loser?"

"Could say that doc. Still thinks he's the wicked smart gunslinger, but it wouldn't matter cause he'd never know where to shoot."

I open my Moleskin to write:

"Stan Still – maybe there is something to what Wilson has been saying. This story about Bernice Brownstone got me thinking about the Tijuana hot rods not being missiles."

A knock comes at the door to Wilson's room. I get up and open it. I see a 35 or so year old looking nerd, with an attempted perfect but still messy part in his hair, wearing a white t-shirt, black wool vest, with Ray Ban Wayfarer frames for his thick eyeglasses:

"Hi doc, am I interrupting?" The slightly built young man asks.

I look over his shoulder. I'm surprised to see a shy but very chic looking pretty dirty blond Italian styled woman with her back to the wall, one foot up on it, wearing a vintage looking raspberry beret. A 1940's looking Leica camera hung around her neck.

"My younger brother Knox, doc, and his gal," Wilson says, not even looking up form his *Carnegie Mellon Today*. "Bring my treats fucker?" He rudely asks his brother.

"Yeah, yeah," the skinny shorter Knox says as he comes into the room, retro black Guess jeans on, crappy pink Vans on without socks, looking like a character out of the 1980's movie *Pretty in Pinky*.

From Knox's side he pulls a messenger bag. I stare in awe at all the art and design pins on its flap, with one that stood out: "Basement Dwellers, Inc." A puny hand was above, like you'd see on the cover of *The Godfather*, pulling the strings. He hands his brother a stack of what look like are *Carnegie Mellon Today* back issues.

I introduce myself.

"Doctor Liam Egan," I say.

I hold out my hand to shake Knox's.

"Knox," he holds out his skinny hand, sporting what looks like an old Swatch watch, not looking me in the eye, but down toward the ground, as he barely shakes my hand.

"You live in New York, son?" I ask as Knox takes his hand from mine.

"Yeah," he looks around his brother's room, "at my parents' pad in Brighton Beach."

Knox then reaches into his bag to pull out a Snicker's bar box, and chucks it to his brother, who doesn't even say thank you when he catches it. As Skip rips open the Snicker's box, I look back to Knox.

"What do you do for a living?" I ask Knox.

He shrugs as he closes his messenger bag. His style looks tame when compared to his brother's long unruly hair and bravado.

"I teach cultural anthropology at Kingsborough Community College," Knox says.

"No Wall Street for you, like your brother?" According to agent Wilson's file, he got a Wall Street job after Carnegie Mellon.

"No," Knox shrugs, "I tried that out after Carnegie, but ditched it at the time to teach, and to work at a start-up."

"What start up is that?"

He shrugs.

"You wouldn't know of it."

"Try me," I say.

"It's called *Dirty French*," Knox says, "we're producing an app."

"What does the app do?"

"Allows virtual petting," he says looking at this brother nonchalantly eat his Snicker's bar.

"Like petting of animals?" I ask.

"Yeah, you can totally pet a dog online."

"Can it piss on you, too?"

"If you don't treat it nice, yeah," Knox says now looking at his brother's biometric sheet. I wonder if Knox can even read it.

"Is the app done?" I ask.

"Nah," Knox bends down to tie his shoes, "still working on it."

"When will you release it?"

He stands back up.

"When it's ready," he says distracted looking out the window.

"Hey, doctor Egan, want a Snicker's bar?" Agent Wilson finally offers, mouth full of a bite, not even offering one to his brother first.

"No thanks."

Agent Wilson then finally throws a bar to his brother, who smiles when catching it, quickly opening it up for eating as if it was going to disappear. As Knox devours the bar, and as agent Wilson lay there slowly eating his in bed, he says to Knox:

"Don't be so stingy, bring two boxes next time."

"Yeah, yeah," says Knox, who starts to walk out the room.

"Nice meeting you, Knox," I say as he walks out the door.

"Ditto, Doc," he says waving his two hands in the air without turning around, "got to head to class now."

I turn to agent Wilson, and want to know more about how he got to be the way he is. It usually starts with those formative teenage years growing up. As he slowly bites into the Snicker's bar, I ask:

"Tell me about your summers as a teen in Brighton. What were they like?"

"They were generally bright, but they weren't always in Brighton cause of those fucking Coney Boys."

"Why, what did they do?"

He shrugs.

"What didn't they do?"

"What do you mean?"

"They were the local street gang of Coney Island, ran the boardwalk over there, and they'd try coming into Brighton to do their tricks, but they'd get pushed back into their shitty pen."

"So what was the problem with them, then?" I ask.

"They started getting desperate, and so instead of trying to hit me or Sash in Brighton, they'd go after Knox on his way back from elementary school."

"These Coney Boys were in high school?"

Wilson shrugs.

"Yeah, they were in high school, and they dealt their shit around Coney."

"So they'd go after Knox instead of you or Sasha," I start to write in my Moleskin, "like how?"

"They'd throw rocks at Knox, chase him through the neighborhood, threaten him that they'd break his hands, face, feet, or our parents' hands, face, feet, if he didn't give them his lunch money, pledge allegiance to the Coney Boys."

Wilson rests the *Carnegie Mellon Today* on his lap to peer at me:

"They got him a few times, bruised him up and stuff, but then me and Sash told Brownie at *Tijuana*."

"Brownie is this Willie Robinson character from the bathroom at *Tijuana*, the one who shepherded you and Sasha's first time?"

"No, the other Brownie," he says sarcastically.

I ignore his tomfoolery.

"So you tell Brownie, and what happened?"

Wilson nonchalantly looks back at his magazine.

"They put some dead rats on the Coney Boys' back porches."

"Who is they?" I ask.

"The ones who ran *Tijuana*."

I wonder if Brownstone was the one who ordered it.

"But the funniest shit," agent Wilson continues, "is when them Coney Boys was about to graduate from Brooklyn College, and they were busted for that shit."

Wilson giggles to himself.

I put my pen down.

"These crimes mentioned in your file?" I ask.

"No, the other crimes," he says then pauses. "Yeah, doc, Brooklyn College admin found all of these photos on the computers of those boys wearing stilts and 'cuddling' with humongous giraffes all on some farm in Upstate New York."

Agent Wilson got a misdemeanor conviction for "aiding and abetting" Sasha's hacking into the Coney Boys' computers. Wilson continued:

"Check the records, and you'd see them Coney Boys got prosecuted for crimes against mother-nature, I think it was a misdemeanor in New York," Wilson says thinking back.

To my surprise, as I browsed at the photos in agent Wilson's Brooklyn criminal file, he was right.

But I wondered if the photos were artfully doctored frauds.

Regardless, they got the job done.

I look back up at Wilson:

"And that's when the Brooklyn District Attorney's office prosecuted you for aiding and abetting Sasha's hacking of those boys' accounts?"

"Yeah, yeah," he waves the misdemeanor conviction away like he was a busy man and couldn't afford the time, "boring bullshit."

"What do you mean?"

"What I mean is that it's all circumstantial evidence they got us on, see, cause whoever hacked those Coney Boys computers used Russian code to frame Sasha."

He picks his nose, ever so slightly, to itch it, like when you are stuck in traffic.

"So I am pretty sure them Coney Boys told them cops that me and Sash did it, what with our prior beef and all, plus Sash's family being Russian and us being at Brooklyn Tech. In isolation, good circumstantial evidence of guilt."

I peer back into his file.

The New York City police report lists agent Wilson's e-mail alias as "Bill Bakes," even though the bbakes@ gmail.com Google e-mail account is registered to Sasha. That's because the cyber detectives found numerous fishing e-mails on the Google e-mail sent to the Coney Boys using the Internet service provider associated with Wilson's home wireless account. The e-mails, according to the police report, used Trojan horse headers "associated with Russian hacking."

I print the aiding and abetting hacking conviction, pick it off the printer behind me, and hold it up to Wilson:

"But you didn't plant this deep fake stuff?" I ask.

He looks up at me, pulls his shades down onto the tip of his nose as if he never saw the conviction before, and gazes into my eyes:

"If I did it, I would tell you, but I didn't. Nor did Sasha. We think it was someone else in Coney Island who had a gripe with them boys at Brooklyn College, and who framed us by registering the Google e-mail in Sasha's name, and then by hopping on my parents' wireless network to send the fishing e-mails to the Coney Boys. We were one massive distraction, I tell you. I'd love to slowly strangle whoever brought the heat on us, cause we never sent any of those e-mails. Fucking bastards whoever did it!"

He throws the magazine on the floor in disgust, then pushes his sunglasses back up on his nose as he recomposes himself.

I didn't believe his malarkey one bit.

I had reviewed numerous e-mails between him and Sasha, with what I knew was, according to the New York City police department, Sasha's alter ego e-mail address of "Bill Bakes"—bbakes@gmail.com -- copied as red herring to throw people off. I saw first hand how they reminisced at and relished what happened to those Coney Boys, like in this e-mail, which was sent while Wilson was in Ukraine, with Wilson using his "Dodgy Bond" alias, and Sasha his "Vodka Jalapeno" alias. I peer at it while sitting next to Wilson:

From: Dodgy Bond
To: Vodka Jalapeno
Cc: Bill Bakes
Date: February 15, 2014
Re: Coney porn!

Dude, remember those fucking Coney idiots, and all-of-their Animal Planet photos they got busted for?

From: Vodka Jalapeno
To: Dodgy Bond
Cc: Bill Bakes
Date: February 15, 2014
Re: Coney porn!

Fucking hilarious. One of the all time best hacks in the history of computing, nyet! Those idiots had no idea what hit them, da. Deep fake shots, big time classic stuff, Chick & Chong would be proud! Guess that boomerang Me So Boring program we created does work?

The e-mails clearly showed that Sasha and agent Wilson had the motive, and clearly the capacity, to commit the Coney Boys' hacking crime. If this *Me So Boring* program worked, as it appeared to judging by the bestial hack into the

Coney Boys' computers, then how did it work? And how did Skip and Sasha work together in a way that wasn't so easily perceived by outsiders?

My curiosity was officially peeked. By the time I look up from my computer, Wilson was fast asleep, mouth open, snoring, black sunglasses resting back on the tip of his nose. I realize that our time was up, and I gather my things together. As I do, I wonder to myself:

Would I end up being the cat that curiosity kills? Or would my curious black cat protect me from the "deep state" supposedly that pushed Wilson into here? Perhaps I'd find out, I thought, during my fourth session with agent Wilson during the Tijuana missile crisis.

/Chapter 4:

BAD MACHO HOMBRE?

"**S**ash and I didn't talk for months after graduating high school, until out of the blue he e-mailed me a video of him dancing to house music with some granny," Wilson says during our next session on the morning of Thursday, October 26, 2017, as he sits on the toilet.

Speaking with Wilson through the bathroom door cause my schedule was cramped, and couldn't wait for him to finish, I crouch down, not like a hidden dragon but more like a confused one, I make the following note in my Moleskin during the silence:

"House music dancing grandma – Bernice Brownstone?"

I pull my laptop out, put it on my lap, and open up Wilson's file. According to the file, after graduating from Brooklyn Tech, Sasha's family moved to Moscow, where he went to the Moscow Technical Institute, "cause his parents decided it was more important to take care of their grandma in Moscow than to run Brooklyn's coffee houses," in agent Wilson's words.

To Director Still, this was all a ploy by Sasha to control Skip. I look down at this e-mail that Still sent to me when introducing agent Wilson's case to me:

> *I don't care how long it was that they didn't talk, cause I know they were conspiring the whole time, probably off line, like in that awful sex filled Central park, with Sasha playing with Skip's heart strings.*

Wilson's diary excerpts seem to support Director Still's narrative.

Here's another entry from when Wilson was in college, and which I pull out and read during Wilson's moment of toilet Zen:

Fuck, I miss that guy so much. Maybe I should have been gay? I mean, I haven't dated in so long, yeah fucks here and there, but these chicks don't make me laugh like Sash. Remembering those midnights on the rooftops, where we put movies up on the brick wall, laughing with the girls, and how he used to look at me with that guilty got away with it grin, makes me so sad.

Another diary entry, this one from while he was also in college, also seemed to support Director Still's deep stated analysis:

Totally got laid this weekend by those hot tamales from Pitt, but they didn't stick around in the morning. Was it my coffee? Weird, cause Sash and I used to be a hit with those girls back in Brooklyn. They'd always call us to get together. We didn't have to make so much effort. I remember Fyodor, Sash's father, a finely dressed looking composer with a super small 1940s looking mustache, saying as he cut the grass: "Da, the good relations with the women is like the shark swimming to breath, cause the relationship either moves forward, or it dies."

Why can't I find those chicks again? Was Sash my Lucky Luciano?

Sitting there in my squat outside of Wilson's bathroom, I wondered whether these were simply two boyhood friends from Brighton who deeply cared for one another? Maybe this was something that was impossible for Director Still, and his "deep state," which agent Wilson called "shallow world," to compute using an outdated Cold War prism through which to view a post-Soviet world?

Suddenly, Wilson says:

"Yeah, so it had been months since graduation, and all of I sudden, I get this totally from left field e-mail from Sash, and it was all like, 'granny got her groove back this week,' and then attached this totally out there video of him dancing, sweaty, his 1940's tight mustache all sweaty, in this Moscow club, and then who comes on the video but this gray haired granny, doing leg kicks in the air, wearing a red beret, sweating all over her blouse, and nodding her head in a be-bop way, with all of these younger men dancing around her, only for her pull out that Zippo lighter and fling its flame into the camera's eye as Sash came on and yelled, with this granny kissing him on the cheek, something like 'Get the fuck out here you idiot, and stop staring at your bellybutton.'"

"So complete radio silence, I mean no phone calls, e-mails, letters, nothing, from the time that you and Sasha graduated from Brooklyn Tech?" I ask through the bathroom door.

Wilson then says:

"That sounds about right, but I am sure that Still said something like it was 'camouflage for off line communications,' or something like that."

True enough, there was a note by Director Still affixed to the granny video e-mail from Sasha to Wilson that said: "they were obviously meeting up in person, don't believe the silence."

Sitting there outside the bathroom, I questioned whether Wilson or Sasha somehow had access to Still's e-mail, because Wilson had some suspicious insights into the inner workings of Still's mind.

Wilson then whispers through the door to screw with me:

"Taught us to think different at Carnegie, but then I get out, and, after joining CIA a few weeks after September 11th, I found out that most people wanted me to think the same, or 'obey,' and that's what got me into trouble, what got me into here, and why I missed Sash's cynical mind so much."

I then ask:

"So you don't think there is anything to Director Still's claim that you and Sasha were conspiring all along to create this Tijuana missile crisis?"

"Still is too caught up in unknown unknowns instead of focusing on the known," Wilson says as I hear him moving over to get some toilet paper. "Known that my family is from Brooklyn, known that my mother is from an old American family whose spies go back to before 1776, known that my grandfather was a legendary Allied spy during WWII, and known that I saw what happened on September 11. But he was so focused on the unknown unknowns he never focused on what he did know, which makes him myopic."

"Cause it gave him a skewed version of the facts?" I ask.

"Skewed to the point where he wouldn't know the truth if it came up and bit him on the ass, cause he'd mistake it for a lie, a deception, something to get him away from his convenient little truths about September 11th only being enabled by those overseas, when they had aiders and abettors right here in America."

"Or he'd mistake the truth as a traitor?"

Wilson then says:

"Yeah, a traitor, because the truth is a traitor to a comforting collective denial of what's real."

Wilson's story of mistaken identity as the enemy isn't totally unheard of. I remember reading about Great Britain's ambassador in Charleston, South Carolina. Right before the Civil War, the Union considered him an enemy even though he was an abolitionist, merely because the Union spies only read his public correspondence -- which understandably catered to his hosts – and not the secret dispatches he sent to the Crown.

I hear the toilet flush as Wilson whispers:

"A-."

I look down to my laptop. I replay the video of Sasha and the grandmother dancing in the Moscow nightclub, with Sasha wearing a custom made looking tuxedo on him. A memory comes back into my head of me visiting New York once and going to this *KGB* bar in the East Village. The Moscow bar in the video and the East Village *KGB* bar, with its red velvet couches and Soviet Union style posters, looked suspiciously similar. Out of curiosity, I look up the *KGB* bar to see if it was running in New York around the time of the video, using Way Back Machine.

"Holy shit," I whisper to myself when I found out it was.

"It wasn't holy," Wilson comments from behind the door, "but it was an A-."

He starts to open the door, and I get up off the ground, laptop in hand, and I walk over to the seat next to his bed, taking the spot on my chair.

As he moves into bed, he zips up his black tracksuit top all the way to the top cause of the strong air conditioning, and I ask:

"Do you think Director Still, or your CIA file," I look down onto my laptop, "make any allowance for the possibility that you maybe see a bulls eye they are blind to?"

I ask this cause agent Wilson's sense of humor is usually a sign of abstract planning in what might appear to be a random setting to the untrained eye, a sign that maybe a deeper plan is afoot when someone is thought of as "crazy," which is what Director Still thinks of agent Wilson.

Wilson shrugs as he picks his *Carnegie Mellon Today* back up, opening up to yet another centerfold like spread. He then says:

"Some in CIA always acted like somehow Carnegie Mellon made a mistake by letting me in, or that my education was all a fraud, merely cause I said things they hated hearing, but which they needed to hear. Reminds me of the quote from Plato, something like 'nobody is more hated than the filthy horny bastard who sometimes speaks dirty truths.'"

"I didn't know Plato said that," I ask.

"For sure, he whispered it in my ear one night," Wilson smirks.

He takes off his sunglasses to clean them. "CIA asked for copies of my Carnegie Mellon transcripts more than once, cause they couldn't believe a guy 'like that' could go to a school 'like that,'" Wilson rested the magazine on his lap as he made quotation marks around "like that." He then inspected the centerfold piece, pointing to one part.

I shrug. I browse through the e-mails from Director Still in Wilson's file, and come across this one, not long after Wilson was admitted on April 16 earlier this year:

> *From: Director Stan Still*
> *To: Dr. Liam Egan*
> *Date: March 9, 2017*
> *Re: Be careful!*
>
> *Doc, just wanted to warn you that Wilson is a great fucking liar, a liar's liar, but has nothing under the paint after you scratch it, just a mindless thug with no self-control. Word has it that he cheated throughout college, had one of his Brooklyn friends, a black guy named Sunny*

Robinson, father's name Willie, go to class for him from Brooklyn, take all of his tests.

Couldn't confirm what Director Still said. When I looked at agent Wilson's stellar Carnegie Mellon grades in his CIA file a few weeks ago, there was no record of cheating or other nefarious conduct.

Curious to get my own input on things directly from one of agent Wilson's professors, I took a train to Pittsburg one weekend in March of this year to talk to Carnegie Mellon professor Dr. Bora Wu, a warm smiling bushy haired mustached man with Mongol eyes, "off the record."

"Come on, that kid was one of the best I had in class," Wu said, sipping a black coffee in his office while reading *Pittsburgh Today*, "don't remember a better student."

I shook my head as I stared at my notes, not able to figure out how all the rumors about Wilson's time at Carnegie Mellon could be so wrong. Then I thought to ask:

"Where did Wilson sit?"

"Usually in the front row," Wu said as he licked his coffee cup, not even looking at me while he did his crossword puzzle.

"Did he usually sit straight up, or tend to slouch in his chair?"

I knew from seeing Wilson at the hospital that he tended to slouch in his bed, with nurses always perking him upward, straightening out his pillow, while he acted like they were disturbing his solitude.

"Eh, um," Professor Wu looked upward towards the star filled ceiling, "he sat up straight," he then got back to his cross word puzzle, occasionally checking the score of the Pirates game that was playing over his junky looking 1980s hand held radio, putting his right hand up to his long pruned ear.

"Straight," I said to myself as I wrote a note in my Moleskin, "odd." I paused again to think for a moment. "Professor Wu, what did Wilson look like in college?"

He paused to look out the window for a moment at a crow flying by then went back to his puzzle.

"Handsome fellow," he said as he made a mark, "very jovial, especially with the ladies," he made another crossword puzzle mark.

"Sort of a ladies man, you would say?" I asked.

"He was no Hugh Hefner, but he wasn't celibate either," the professor said with a sly smirk on his face.

"Did you ever hear any rumors about Wilson, anything out of the ordinary, of criminal conduct?" I asked.

"Oh yeah," he nodded, "word has it he sold recreational drugs to most of the students," he snapped his fingers, "and I think I remember hearing something about *Risky Business* parties."

I finally was on to something! A breakthrough in this fog of rumors I was sifting through. I got my pen ready to write, and leaned over to the professor:

"How did you know all this, who told you?"

He mumbled to himself as he made some more notes on the crossword puzzle, seeming like he didn't even hear what I was saying.

"Professor," I leaned over even closer to him, "how did you know about these *Risky Business* parties?"

"What? Oh, yeah, I think it was in one of the bathrooms that I overheard some students talking about them."

"Remember who those voices were from?"

He looked over at me, seemingly exhausted by my question:

"Come on, doc, I was sitting in a bathroom stall concentrating on something more important," he then went back to his crossword puzzle.

I wrote down in my notebook, "potential drug and sex brokering, but unconfirmed – follow up with patient." I then asked the professor:

"Do you remember Wilson having dark skin?"

"Dark like a mocha latte or real dark like black coffee?" Dr. Wu asked.

"Black coffee," I said.

"No," he said, making another mark on his crossword puzzle.

"Okay, mocha latte dark?"

He sipped some of his coffee, looked at it like he was seeing a long lost love, then said:

"I can't live without it."

"Yeah, but was Wilson's skin color in college like a mocha latte?"

He made a thirsty look at the coffee, Pittsburgh Pirates game roaring in the background:

"Sort of."

I looked up at him from my notes.

"Sort of? What do you mean?"

"What I mean," he looked over at me through his big clear boxy glasses, the type you might have seen on a Lou Wasserman, "is that his skin was like a mocha latte, but only if you are talking about a tall sized one with gluten free milk," he did an almost imperceptible smirk.

I stared at Professor Wu. I then peered down into my booklet and wrote:

"Holy shit!"

And so, sitting here months later on this October 26th, staring at Agent Wilson's stark white skin in his hospital room, I look down onto my Moleskin from that "holy shit" day with Professor Wu. I then flip through Wilson's CIA file, and glance again at the rest of Director Still's e-mail from March 9, 2017:

Also, Russian hackers circumvented CIA's coded digital firewall just after Wilson joined the Agency in 2001, and tampered with the information in his file. So who knows what's real in there, and what's complete unadulterated horse manure you'd find in a soap opera, you know? Be careful, this guy is a big charlatan.

Yours, SS.

I look up at Wilson, who is peeking through *Carnegie Mellon Today*, and ask:

"Did you know Director Still thinks this Sasha hacked your CIA files?"

He slowly turns the page of the magazine and then he says:

"Yeah, and?" He turns the cloud storage centerfold photo around to show me.

I wave it away. He shrugs, not understanding why I'm not interested.

"Do you know why CIA suspected your Russian friend of getting into your file?"

"Because his coded Russian fingerprints badly wanted penetration into my file full of juicy adventures," he slowly says with an inscrutable smirk.

I write into my Moleskin:

"Something to what Still says? Patient doesn't deny that Sasha is Russian hacker, nor that Russian code was used."

I look back at Wilson and then write this down in my Moleskin:

"Wilson – dirty lying smuggler."

"Golly, doc, I think it's time, right, for us to part ways?" Wilson says and points to the clock on the wall. He is right. Our time is up. I gather my things and say as I do:

"Right, right, get some rest."

"Ditto doc, ditto," he says as I walk out the room. I turn off the light and hear the faint sound of a baseball game on his little hand held radio after I close the door to his room. Later that night, I get back home to sleep all of the drama off from the day and let it simmer during my day off.

Two days later, on October 31, 2017, around 7:00 a.m., I arrive at my office, close my door, and receive this e-mail from *The New York Times* about cyber-bullying:

CYBER BULLYING ON THE RISE
SHOCKING?

As I read the article about how people treat other people online, much unlike how we treat people in person, I think about what Wilson said about the Coney Boys going after Knox: "They'd throw rocks at him, chase him through the neighborhood, threaten him that they'd break his hands, face, feet, if he didn't give them his lunch money."

Sitting back in my chair, I look up to the ceiling, and whisper out loud: "Maybe Wilson looks like a dirty lying smuggler, talks like one, but maybe he isn't always one?" I look back down onto the article about cyber bullying, and write down into my Moleskin, "if Wilson is such a bad macho hombre, why didn't he leave Knox, his super gay looking brother, to those Coney wolves and say, 'yuck, super gay'?"

Loud knocks on my office door take me out of my thoughts.

/Chapter 5:

(BEAUTIFUL, USELESS, IDIOTS_

"Wilson is going mad, the chap is about to jump out the window," Otis, the 91 yea   r old or so witch white skinned janitor, says in his thick English accent through my office door at about 7:30 a.m.

I quickly get up out of my chair, grab my satchel stashed with my computer and needles, and rush over to Wilson's room, where I hear him screaming this down the hall: "net, net, get them a net, where is the fucking net, get them a net, they are jumping, don't you see, jumping, no net, where's the fucking net?"

I presume he is having a bad dream about seeing the jumpers on September 11th.

But when I open the door to his room, he is sitting upright with his dark sunglasses on, arms crossed.

He looks over at me:

"Who is making all of that crazy racket?"

"What the fuck, Wilson? It's like 7:30 a.m."

He pulls open his covers, zips down his top to get more comfortable, and says, "yeah, well, I wanted to talk to you about something, it's important," CNN blared in the background:

PRESIDENT SEAGULL'S
TIJUANA
MISSILE CRISIS SPEECH

"What is it, couldn't it have waited?" I ask him again as I take off my glasses, and sit next to his bed.

"Maybe, but then again, maybe not," he looked up to the television as President Seagull spoke.

"Okay, alright," I wave submissively at agent Wilson. "What's is it?" I grab the old cup of coffee that I had left next to him, with the black straw in it.

"Want to tell you doc, why I got into all of this," he looks around the hospital room like it was new to him.

I sip more cold coffee, and begrudgingly say, "alright Wilson, lay it on me."

"Joined CIA to get laid," he says with a straight face, watching the news.

"Would have been better off going to Hollywood if you wanted that," I say back to him, watching the news with him.

"Yeah, but they wouldn't have appreciated my hot rod tech skills out there," he says.

I pull my Moleskin out of my bag. I tap my pen on the notebook, and then open it up to take some notes.

"But seriously, doc, it was seeing them folks jumping on September 11th that got me into this shit, folks like my pop's friend Eddie from Staten Island, just a janitor, didn't do anything."

"You never really told me about that day, although I read about it in your diaries," the cold black coffee in my mouth tasting kind of like the smoke must have tasted in downtown Manhattan on September 11th.

"Saw it all go down from my rooftop," Wilson says, turning the television off but then flipping on his small portable radio to the jazz station. "Cause I was living blocks away from the World Trade Center, and heard the first plane hit," he looks over at me through his sunglasses, which he uses as a wall, just like anger, to keep people at bay.

"What did you think when you heard the first one hit?"

John Coltrane's *Giant Steps* plays in the background over the radio.

"Heard the sonic boom, that was the first one that hit, but I saw the second one hit the second tower, and knew it was some kind of attack."

"By Russian hackers?" I ask with my wry Irish smirk.

"Who else would it be?" He chuckles.

"I read your diary entry about that, and I know how it affected you." The diary entry, dated sometime in late September of 2001, read as follows:

> *Little specks of dust, dust in the wind, flowing like they had no control over where they were going, or where they came from, fire from the building, smoking all over, and all I could do was be thankful I wasn't one of them, or one of their family members. But I was also so angry that I couldn't do anything, sitting there in my fancy apartment, with my fancy job as an analyst at a private equity firm, and getting my fancy salary. I felt like a big fucking loser.*

Glaring at Wilson, I say:

"So 9/11 prompted you to join CIA?"

"Yeah," he nods yes.

"And what about Sasha, when did he join the Russian CIA?"

"Russian CIA is like an oxymoron, doc," he says.

"Right, you know what I mean."

"Yeah, well, he joined sometime after that Moscow subway bombing, which was in March of 2010, I think."

But my conditioned doubts about Wilson creep back in almost involuntarily:

"So, come on, why did you really join CIA?"

He shakes his head, slightly annoyed.

"It doesn't matter why I tell you I joined, and it doesn't matter why you believe I joined, cause there is that file you've been looking at on your laptop," he adjusts himself in his bed as he pulls out an old *Mad Magazine* from the stack of reading materials next to his bed, "all of the rumor and hype about me can't make the truth disappear, but such things can make it nearly impossible to find."

"Rumors and smears?" I ask sipping the old coffee as the little old stereo boomed *Blue Skies* by Benny Goodman.

"Yeah, yeah," he nods over to me, sunglasses sitting on the tip of his nose, "like me being some evil hacking crook from Brooklyn."

"But you are a hacking crook from Brooklyn," I say.

He looks back at the *Mad Magazine*, and, as he intently reads, he says:

"Yeah, but whose to say I am the evil one? Nobody seems to understand 'Brooklyn camouflage,'" he dropped the *Mad Magazine* down put quotations around "Brooklyn camouflage."

"Is that some sexual position?" I ask.

"Yeah, only with parrots," he picks the mag back up.

"Brooklyn camouflage – what is it?" I write down in my Moleskin.

"Got to use the John again, doc, be right back," he then says while I am writing, and as I get a peek at his matching Fila track suit bottom draping on his surprisingly well manicured toes.

Then I catch myself, wait a minute, this fucking guy!

Gets me in here in start of the morning and then acts like I have to wait for him.

But there was something that made me want to stay. Maybe there was a crack in Director Still's analysis of the Tijuana situation that nobody saw because they were drowning in the cacophony of rumored facts that might make us feel good – except for outliers like agent Wilson, who kept those fake news facts at bay to see the sinister dark forest that is a fact of life's yin-yang?

So a very small part of me wondered if there was another shockingly professional side to Wilson that wasn't in CIA's report.

To find it, I had to dig through Wilson's diary entries from whenever he was attending class at Carnegie Mellon about his former sweetheart, named Nika Shostakovich:

> *Saw another photo of Nika and her Aryan youth looking boyfriend from Massachusetts today in The New York Times, and I was sort of happy, but I was also sort of sad. Underneath the photo it said something like, "Nika, Brooklyn, NY, and Rich Barks, Boston, Massachusetts, drink fresh lemonade in Southampton on a hot summer day." Thing is, I could see something in her eyes, something that didn't mirror her smile. That sadness in her eyes, that darkness, is something that I saw in the first photo of her and this Rich Barks in some Hamptons paper, same smile, but same dark eyes. Given my Bobby Fishy ways, I knew there was something fishy about Bohne, something down below which I sensed. Can't explain it, frustrating, but I feel something horrible is there.*

What was it that Wilson saw?

I sit there wondering in his hospital room. Some doubt we have that sixth sense, thinking that all we need to know is out in the open. But from what my pop told me, Einstein said something like: "The intuitive mind is a sacred gift, and the rational mind is its servant, but we have created a world where the intuitive mind takes a back seat to the servant, which is like having a stunning woman you are about to make out with in the dark bedroom, but the rational mind keeps wanting to turn on the light cause its afraid of what may happen in the dark, which would screw up the mood, see boy?"

Over the years, I've had enough experience treating spies to know that there is much our rational minds can't fathom, likely because the Gods to honest truth is oftentimes too overwhelming, or disturbing, to our cozy feel good simplistic understanding of the world. So as Wilson sits on the toilet, I turn a few pages forward in his diary from when he was at Carnegie Mellon:

> *Seeing Nika in those papers and not being able to do anything about who I think she is with makes me crazy, cause I know something fishy about him, but she doesn't want to talk anymore, nothing. Maybe that's cause I know that Rich Barks been beating her, abusing her, doing things to her that she doesn't talk about, stores away in the deep recesses of her mind. Nobody would believe me if I told them, would think I was crazy, so been keeping my mouth shut, smoking more, and getting back into – who would have known? – shop lifting from fancy shops for a few months now. Finally got pinched last week after months of lifting things after smoking, and it was only when I was on the inside that I finally got some relief from another beautiful, useless, idiot.*

Turn his diary a few pages, and peer at this one:

> *Locked in the Pittsburgh Central Jail for a few two days sucked, but what do you know? I got to meet some amazing cats. One white haired old guy with a big Santa Claus beard who was sitting next to me, whiskey on his breath, was great to talk to, cause I told him everything I'd*

seen about Nika's boyfriend Rich, how I felt there was some dark demons in that man, in his eyes, maybe cause he had something happen to him when he was a young Catholic man in Boston, because those who've been hurt as kids oftentimes have a demon impregnated inside that hurt their kids—or their partners. And, like fake news, it goes from generation to generation until the corrupted code is corrected. I felt, in my soul, Rich was doing to the same thing to Nika, or would do the same things to her, and would do the same to their children if they had any.

Never forget how this tall pirate patched man, Jesse Hardin, with an unruly beard just sat there, picking his nose, like he wasn't listening, looking around as I blabbed to him, picking up his ass to fart here and there, only for him to finally say, after me spilling the beans to him about what I thought was going on, he put his hand on my shoulder, he burps, then said:

"Young man, gone not done need tell you that you know exactly who this here Rich Barks is, what he does, cause the eyes don't dang lie none, son, only mouths do, so why you not trusting yourself more? Downright obvious to me she hiding from you cause you know the deeper dark truth about him, and I am just a country boy, not smart like you," his long fingers and big palm patted me on the shoulder. "But I reckon things like this have a way of working themselves out, dig me now?" he said to me.

And I said: "what do you mean?"

And he said something like: "kind of like how them courts decide if something is porn or not, you'll know it when you see it."

Right then, Wilson flushes the toilet. He comes out of the bathroom.

"Interesting reading?" He asks.

"Was reading about your meeting with this hillbilly Jesse in Pittsburgh's central jail."

"One trippy dude, that Jesse, cause his eye could read me without me saying a word, or maybe I didn't understand him at all and he was talking about his brother, cause he had the thickest country accent I've ever heard."

"So what ever happened to Nika Shostakovich and this Rich Barks?"

Wilson shrugs. He puts his vampire glasses on the table, lets his long hair drip over his shoulders, and curls up in a fetal position. With his eyes closed, he says:

"Don't know, I gave up after all that drama, cause all that thinking about her and feeling like a loser for not being able to do anything got me to let go."

He takes off his tracksuit top off and throws it over towards the chair.

"Getting tired, doc, maybe taking the shit took the energy out of me, could we pick this up next session?" He looks up to me.

This guy was too much. Got me out of my office with his screaming and now pulls this malarkey? But I took some deep breaths.

"Yea, Wilson," I start gathering my laptop and coffee, "no problem. We'll pick up next time."

I sort of pat him on his shoulder. I could tell it calms him. He seems to get faster to sleep. I left his room and closed the door.

When I get back into my office, I realize I never understood what Wilson meant by "Brooklyn camouflage." That got me to thinking of what happened to this Rich Barks from Boston, who was dating agent Wilson's college sweetheart. So I open up Google on my desktop, enter "Rich Barks," and an article from page 6 of *The New York Post* pops up from July 27, 1997, not long after Skip graduated from Carnegie Mellon:

HIGH ROLLER
RICH BARKS
EATEN BY LION
ON SAFARI IN KENYA?

My mouth goes agape. I read down below in the article how:

Mr. Bohne was last seen near the part of the park where lions, giraffes, and other wildlife were known to come up to visitor vehicles. To determine if there was potential foul play, investigators searched his computer and believe they found photos of men with obviously under aged boys. While they investigate, we spoke to one Luther Wolf, of Casper, Wyoming, who was on safari with his California tech company in Kenya at the time. According to Mr. Wolf, "totally saw this guy naked one night running into the darkness around camp. I first thought it was some baby elephant, but then I realized it was some butt naked man. I was like: what the crud? That's when I screamed bloody murder and called the cops?"

Leaning back into the chair, I look up and wonder whether Wilson's Brooklyn apparently self-destructive camouflage was a brain wavelength. I also wondered whether he sometimes used this idiocy not for "worse than deplorable behavior," as Director Still had told me, but for producing artwork only "beautiful, useless, idiots like Sasha," as he said in one diary entry, "could see."

Suddenly, I get this e-mail from Director Still. It reads:

How's the sessions coming along, doc? We are big time eager beaver here to get a move on, cause who knows what's going to happen, you know? Anyway, watch out for that crafty cockroach you have in your care, cause that's what happened when we sent him to that God damned Afghanistan—he survived like a crafty cockroach! Let me know, doc, ASAP.

I thought to myself: what's a "crafty cockroach"? Perhaps, I thought, I'd find out during my next session with Wilson, our sixth during the Tijuana crisis, on November 2, 2017.

/Chapter 6:

!STONER HOUDINI.\

"I pulled the huge thing out of my pants and the Afghan warlords' eyes lit up," Wilson says after I ask him: "what's a crafty cockroach?"

"They couldn't believe how wrinkled your huge thing was?" I sip my coffee next to Wilson's bed during our morning session a week later.

"They probably couldn't believe it's ghostly color either," he smirks while he plays with his loose ends.

I look down at my laptop on the chair next to me. I stare at Wilson's diary entries surrounding his Afghan "mission." Many entries affixed hacked e-mails Sasha farmed from Director Unger and Assistant Director Chris Madison. I know the e-mails were hacked cause agent Wilson's file says they found Russian digital fingerprints all over Langley's servers. The following e-mail from Director Unger to Assistant Director Madison which was cut and pasted into Wilson's diary, is informative:

> From: Stan Still
> To: Chris Cross
> Re: Taking out the trash
> Date: September 27, 2015
>
> Get this little prick troublemaker over to Kabul, and tell him we are sending him on an important mission to camp in the mountains out-side the city, high up, for him to do recon on the Afghan warlords. We'll send the warlords some message that he's going to be up there, where he

is, from one of our proxies over there, and then we can horse trade for some info using his shitty short life. They'll skin him alive!

> *From: Chris Cross*
> *To: Stan Still*
> *Re: Taking out the trash*
> *Date: September 27, 2015*

Little prick won't know what hit him. LOL!

I look up at agent Wilson. He is still inspecting his ratty loose ends. I peek down at his diary entry from September 29, 2015, after he found out CIA was sending him to Afghanistan:

> *Whoa! I'm getting a free trip to Afghanistan! Director Still told me today that I have a "special mission" over there, doing some recon on some Afghan warlord. Course, I know its all bullshit, and they are trying to hang me. But whatever! I've never been to Afghanistan, and just bought a Lonely Planet traveler book on the sights, including some fancy coffee shop in Kabul that's supposed to be mad tits. They got to have the best hash in the world. Stoked! I'll get to try out my mini-hookah, which is still so extra virgin.*

I look up and ask Wilson:

"You weren't scared one bit about going over there?"

He peers over at me, drops his sunglasses on the edge of his nose like my granny used to do when she'd review my homework, and slowly says:

"Should I have been?"

I shrug and open up Google maps to see where he was dropped off in the Afghanistan's Kona Coffee Valley.

"Yeah," I nod as I look at the map, "you should have been scared." I then crouch down to make a note in my Moleskin:

"Patient – shows extreme denial in dangerous situations. Maybe Stan Still was right – Wilson is bipolar-schizophrenic, imagining safety when it's not there, his own worst enemy."

"Well," agent Wilson pushes his sunglasses back up on his nose. He opens up another Snicker's bar from his stash. As he chomps on it, he says: "I was super excited."

"Do you see where they dropped you?" I turn around my laptop to show him.

"Doc, yeah, I see where they dropped me, cause I was there when they dropped you."

He smirks. I turn my computer back around.

"Says here in your file it was in the middle of the night that they dropped you in that valley?"

"More like in the morning, twilight hour, between night and day."

"What did you bring with you?"

"GI Joe action figures and some Barbie dolls to mate them with."

"Come on, Wilson, I'm being serious, I have to leave soon," I look at my watch.

He picks some peanut out of his mouth, inspects it like he did with his loose end, and thinks out loud after slipping it back in his mouth, looking at the ceiling:

"Was one of the prettiest skies I had ever seen in my life, and even the heaviness of my backpack, and my weapons, didn't take away from that morning star, planet Venus, sky that looked down on me that morning."

"Says here it was sometime in October, so must have been chilly?"

He looks over at me, almost pissed that I took him out of his reverie.

"Wasn't Palm Springs hot, I can tell you that, doc."

"So they plop you down, in the middle of the morning, and what did you do?"

He shrugs as he peers at the Snicker's bar nutrient section, briefly taking a moment to review his speed bump belly, worried maybe that the bar would ruin his two-pack. He then says:

"I high tailed it out of the drop spot, and headed up to my camp spot, got my tent set up, and then turned him on."

"Who's him?"

He points over the old Sony hand held radio that was next to the bed.

"You brought that fucking radio up there Wilson?" I hold my pen on my Moleskin, not believing he could be that much of an idiot, as I look over at his crappy 1980s hand held radio.

"Doc, yeah, bring it everywhere, it's like my good luck charm, my pop gave it to me when I was younger, a hand me down."

"He gave it to you used?"

"Yeah, almost nothing he gave me was new, either his clothes, like this track suit," he tugs at it, "or that radio."

"That thing? How could you get reception up in those mountains?"

"Some of the younger Afghans have bootleg stations, spinning Muddy Waters tracks, cause supposing they got bored of their Afghan stuff."

"And how did you know that, Wilson?"

He looks back at me as he puts some Original Chap Stick on his lips and slowly says:

"Girls got to have her their beauty secrets, doc."

I wave off his foolishness.

"Get your secrets at the .99 cent store?" I ask him, pointing my pen at his Chap Stick.

"Only place I go for these and these," he holds up the Snicker's bar and Chap Stick.

As he does, I smirk as I humorously reflect on how Still and Cross attempted to bullshit this obvious expert bullshit artist into getting himself killed. Anever

"Right," I look down on my notes about him being "paranoid schizophrenic."

I cross the two words out.

But I still hold open the possibility that Wilson is a bi-polar depressive.

"So you got your camp all set up, with your radio on, and what are you doing the next day when you get up?"

"Doing my job. I got my telescope out, and put it on top of the ridge, pointing at the large Afghan camp down below."

"To spy on the warlord?"

"Yeah," Wilson says, "he had a great ass."

I smirk.

"And you wrote diary entries, I can see," I say as I look down on Wilson's file.

"Yeah."

"Copy, so you are sitting there in your camp, day in and out?"

"For a few days."

"And you don't think they saw you?"

He moves himself in the bed from his back to his side.

"I know they saw me."

"Come again?"

"Yeah," he nods as he closes his eyes, "I know they saw me."

"How do you know?"

"Cause I made a fire the first night I was there, and brought some mini amps for the radio, so I could hear the music better when I cooked."

Here is why I kept open my diagnosis of him being bi-polar, as many bi-polar types engage in risky business, whether it is shoplifting or otherwise, while in denial of how risky the business is.

"So you are sitting in the mountains, overlooking an 'Afghan warlord Disneyland set up,' as you say here in your diaries, and what did you see?"

"Kids playing on crappy old Soviet looking horses, and they were sitting around a big circle with a hookah smoking and talking and throwing food at one another, probably because the warlord's jokes sucked, so he got to blame his underlings."

"You could see the warlord?"

"Yeah, sitting there, smiling, long beard, watching as the men cussed at the ones who didn't laugh, and I could tell he knew how absurd the whole thing was."

"You were using your scope to see all of this, wrote everything you did down?"

"Yeah, used my scope, but didn't write everything I did down. There are some things I didn't even confess to Still or Cross."

"What's one of them? That you used to be a woman?"

"Maybe," he shrugs as his hands rest close to his cheek, "a wicked broad like Brownstone," he smiles. "But that wasn't it."

"So, what's the thing you didn't confess?"

He shrugs, looks at his fingernails, as though he needed a manicure.

"One night, I went down when their Disney camp was all asleep, and I put some thumbnail sized bugs up on the tents and in the dirt in and about the tents."

"Wouldn't they have heard you?"

"I used some long antennas that I packed to place the bugs on the tents as I sat in the brush from about 40 or so yards away."

"Inventive fellow you are, Wilson."

He smirks again.

"I don't try, but it comes anyway."

"I wish mine worked that way," I look down to my crotch.

He chuckles, and I could see his eyes behind his sunglasses sparkling.

"And so how did you get caught?"

I use quotation marks around "caught." The more I got to know agent Wilson, the more I realized why I used those quotation marks. A bullshit artist like him doesn't get caught unless he wants to get caught.

"Was sitting there one night, eating some rice and beans around the fire, listening to *The Doors* and all of a sudden I felt a long knife go up against my face."

"Alright, so you got the knife against your face, and these Afghans aren't going to take you to Coney Island for a Nathan's?"

"Almost as good as that," he nods and closes his eyes like he needs a moment of silence.

I look down at his diary on my laptop, and read an entry from late November 2015, which he entered after he got back from Afghanistan. It reads:

> *So these cats took me down to their Disney camp, and they are speaking to me in their Pashtun dialect, and I'm just nodding like "what the fuck do you want me to say, dudes?" They are slapping me in the face when I'd don't answer, me smiling like the sick fuck that I am, and they don't understand it, face all bloody, that I got this smirk on it, and they keep looking at each other the more they slap, and hit.*

> *Funny cause they didn't know I had my ear bud inside, with an artificial intelligence software*

that me and Sash developed which translated everything they said, but also told me how to speak in their language, albeit so fucking amateur style. So I had all of the goods on what they were saying, them thinking I didn't know squat, when I knew it all. I think the thing that freaked them out the most is when I started speaking their language and telling them things about their wives, who they were talking about having secret crushes on, who they thought was getting overweight, and how they were going to treat their son's new rash that recently broke out.

They didn't know I had been listening to them for days on end. I know one of their sons was deathly ill from an infection.

"How do you know how to speak?" I remember the main warlord asking, petting his beard like he just got it trimmed at a Brighton Beach Super Cuts.

I shrugged. I remember looking at my nails, all fucked up and dirty, as if they were prim like one of those prim broads at Tijuana, and said something in his native tongue like:

"Got laid with this Afghan girl back in Brooklyn, when I was young, and never forgot it, cause she was one of the best in bed I've ever been with."

The warlord then pondered to himself with sort of sick madman surprise. I think I took him out of his thinking when I said:

"Take this vial of pills from my pocket," I

remember saying in their Pashtun dialect, shitty cause I didn't have any training, "and tell your son to take one in the morning, one at night," I said with the blood dripping down my mouth.

The men looked at each other, started talking about how I was the greatest Satan, cause they left me there with some of their local stew for the night, in some barn with some goatsd, and me just sitting there in my blood, with my hands hog tied behind my back.

Next day, they came and got me in the morning, and they were kissing my bloody cheeks, with one praising how the n pills I gave them helped their son's infection. They cleaned me up, took off my hog tie, and I asked them if I could pull something out.

Warlord said in Pashtun "so long it's not your fast food., tsd"

I pulled the California a bud out and when they saw it, they held it up, and they couldn't believe such a young strain would have that color. It was like some piece of art to them. It was even more of a piece of art when we all smoked it that night, putting it in my little hookah, under the stars, around the fire, with the goats in the background.

I look up at Wilson, whose eyes are still closed, with my mouth sort of agape. I couldn't believe this guy lying there on his side in the bed was able to pull off some stoner Houdini like that.

"So were you finally able to use your Lonely Planet?" I ask.

"I didn't need to," he says with his eyes closed. "They provided me with escorts to show me around Kabul, even took me for some rounds in the mountain range."

I peak back down at agent Wilson's file, at an e-mail from Assistant Director Madison to Director Unger:

> *From: Chris Cross*
> *To: Stan Still*
> *Re: Taking out the trash*
> *Date: November 1, 2015*
>
> *This crafty cockroach is back! God damn it. How the fuck did he get out of that Valley, Stan? Where were our guys? I want an investigation into agent Wilson, what he did over there, we should be able to find some rules that he broke so that we can get him prosecuted for colluding with Afghan warlords, that little schizophrenic paranoid traitorous pecker.*

I look back up at Wilson.

"Looks like Unger and Madison were happy to see you back?"

Wilson just nods slowly, then says:

"Elated."

"What did you tell them that pissed them off so much?" I asked.

He shrugs casually, then says:

"That the Afghan warlord told me Trojan horse sleeper cells were planted throughout the United States before September 11th."

I look over at the almost asleep Wilson. I think to myself: then again, engaging in risky business is what many consider to be bravery when one acts not in denial of the risk, but in spite of it. I then ask.

"Trojan horse?"

"Yeah," he wipes some spit from his mouth with his tracksuit top, "like one big poison pill camouflaged as medicine."

"Since before September 11th?" I ask.

He takes his sunglasses off, getting ready for sleep, as he softly says:

"They thought I was paranoid schizophrenic."

"And that's how you ended up here?"

"It . . . was . . . the . . . start . . . of . . . it," the stoner Houdini peeks through his almost closed eyes, and then he suddenly crashes, starting to snore.

I slowly get up, put the covers over Wilson, and then exit the room. I could see why Director Still thought Wilson wasn't all there, because part of me thought he was partially mad, too. But when I get back into my office and did some digging, I found out that Still did believe at least some of Wilson's findings about the terror cells and even ordered special ops missions outside the U.S. against them, but never against the domestic cells Wilson said he reported. And yet even the overseas missions that Still did order based on Wilson's intelligence, or strategy suggestions, weren't in his file.

Why weren't they?

/CHAPTER 7:

/·JOEY'S

July 4, 1996

*"Word has it that those Murder Inc. guys
still around, and that she runs with them," remember Sasha leaning over and whispering to
me as we sat on the Brighton boardwalk watching Brownstone and her roundtable do a meeting
one morning.*

Sitting in my office during the early morning of Tuesday,
November 7, 2017, I read the words above in Wilson's diary
from when he was at Carnegie Mellon to get ready for my
next session with him. As I stare at the word "disappear"
in Wilson's diary, I started to think important missions and
facts favorable to him were intentionally omitted from his
file. Then I look out the window of my office and think back
to all those things my pop used to tell me about old pappy
George B. Egan, one of my family patriarchs, who used to
quietly run Boston before Joe Kennedy was even born.

Old pappy Egan was allegedly the biggest smuggler in
U.S. history.

But you've never heard of him.

As my pop Hank Egan liked to say, he was "a quiet
Kennedy." Remember my pop saying over oatmeal to me
one morning in our Hyde Park, Chicago home before he
went to teach at the University of Chicago, and as he read
about rising murder rates the *Chicago Tribune*: "son, word
has it that those boys in Murder Inc. mimicked a lot of pappy
Egan's disappearing acts."

Then I remember my pop looking at me, his spectacles dripping from his nose:

"Don't think any of it was true, see. But I'm thinking that, if it was true," he looked back to the article in the *Tribune*, "he'd be able to make all this senseless violence in the city disappear," he turned the paper to show me the headline:

MURDER RATES
UP 72%
IN CHICAGO

"Now why would you say a thing like that, pop?" I remember asking him at the time, as I was a curious high school student who wrote for the school paper, inspired by my old man's hard boiled reporting for *The New York Times* in 1960s Gotham City.

"Cause the wolves run from the dead carcass, son," he said calmly with the cigarette dangling from his mouth, "when the bears come for their meat." I remember my mother, Este, shaking her head in a "here we go" type of way as she ate grapefruit.

"Intense," I remember quietly saying as I looked down at my Irish steel cut oatmeal.

"Yeah, well, son," my pop said as he dripped some of his cigarette ash into the old pappy Egan's black oyster ash tray, "Mother Nature isn't exactly a pompous glove wearing queen from Beverly Hills, and I didn't make her so."

Memories of my pop fade as I peer back at Wilson's diary entry after he got back from Afghanistan in late 2015. It reads:

The Afghans don't much respect women, but they would have respected Brownstone, cause in some ways she was like those unexpected massive swells along California's shores, where you are swimming and don't see them coming, but are forced to duck under them when they do. I never thought the Afghans were "backward" as much as they were just real about power. They respected that wave, the raw physical power that the wave had, and they didn't think women had it.

But, then again, they never met Brownstone.

And so when I saw this shock and awe strategy of President Rush into Crack to oust President Sandy Hussy, I couldn't help but think when I got back from Afghanistan that Brownstone's what I like to call "white widow" disappearing acts get more done, at a fraction of the price, but with no press. President Rush reminded me of Sonny Corleone in the Godfather, good hearted but rushing to do without thinking things through, unlike Michael, who got his street fight ways by learning how to "white widow" whisper.

When I come to the end of Wilson's entry, I peek through some others and find another, dated June 6, 2009, where he talks about the same "white widow" disappearing acts as being the real way to "street fight." I do some word searches through Wilson's file on my lap top, including ones like "white widow" and "street fight," and find this one from Assistant Director Madison to director of the CIA at the time, Ray Gunn, dated June 27, 2009. It says:

By the way, got your message today, and I agree. We have to start being more proactive in seeking out overseas targets and eliminating them in a street fight way, the way that I think some of those Brooklyn monsters used to do it, instead of using shotguns to kill overseas mosquitos.

Sitting there, I was shocked.

On the one hand, they were making Wilson out to be nut job in his official CIA file. But, on the other hand, they were apparently adopting the very strategies he was in favor of in his diary entries like the one above.

I recall Director Cross saying to me:

"After he got back from Afghanistan, Wilson said to me how we should look behind us before we rush to attack those outside in places like Crack, or else we'll end up like Sonny in the *Godfather*, cause, in his view, there were boogey men in our backyard. Can you see how delusional this Wilson is?"

But they didn't think Wilson so delusional that they discounted him completely.

How could they be so two faced? And why?

I put my pen to my chin. I thought it may have all been because of ego, like when your kid tells you something you don't want to believe, especially when your kid is one of those smart asses who corrects the adults, but you end up moving along and following the kid's advice. But you never tell him about it so he "doesn't get too big for his britches."

Thing is, agent Wilson told me he gave them intelligence on numerous domestically based non-profit and religious organizations that were funneling money to various terrorist organizations around the world. But they pretty much ignored it all, meanwhile taking advantage of his strategy suggestions overseas cause, according to one of Assistant Director Madison's few e-mails that addressed the issue:

> *We can't muddy up the waters here too much, cause, if what he says is true, we have a body full of problems, and we just can't have that, cause it will lead to a public panic. Plus, I think*

it's a bunch of paranoid bullshit. Anyway, better to deal with the cancers outside the body that can cause more cancers in the body before we deal with the imaginary ones the body already supposedly has. Otherwise we'll be wasted.

And yet I couldn't get the following diary entry out of my head from Wilson, the one that both of his directors apparently ignored, perhaps because it was easier to keep the simplistic but unrealistic us-versus-them going without thinking there is some of "them" in "us," as agent Wilson pointed out here:

The Afghan warlord told me about the cells they had all throughout the U.S., and which had, in his words, used "Western turn the other cheek respect every religion philosophy against itself," so that anybody who tried to speak out about obvious Trojan horses planted in the United States, who never had any intent on assimilating but were put there with the intention of taking over and intimidating the culture, something that wouldn't be allowed in Iran or China or Saudi Arabia, into racists, crazy people, and uncivilized barbarians.

And I remember the warlord giggling, cause he said something like "I respect barbarians more than these civilized Western idiots, cause at least barbarians see things as they are, and not as they wish them to be. It's why I respect men like you," he smacked me on the shoulder as my long beard shook at the power of his smack, "cause you see how blind your own countrymen can be to their own stupidity, and yet I'll bet they will think of you as the crazy one."

He laughed out loud as he played with his beard. We smoked some more, and drank some tea to his son's recovery. But the conversation never left my memory, which is why I write about it here.

I look at my watch.
Wilson's next session is minutes away.
Before I leave, I peek at Director Still's interpretation of Wilson's entry above:

See, Dr. Egan? This is why this Wilson needs therapy, and a lot of it. Obvious he was brain-washed by this Afghan warlord to think there are malevolent cells in our midst. What a whacko! I'm looking forward to getting him some thera-py so we can finally hang his ass. Or maybe we just send him on another suicide mission – this time making sure it works! I think Kiev will do the trick. We'll send this useful idiot to die when he tries to kill Joey So-So.

When I finish reading, I close the computer, gather my things, and head into Wilson's room. I find him sitting upright in his bed reading a *Carnegie Mellon Today* alumni magazine, jazz blasting over his little worthless looking radio.
"Hey stranger," he says nonchalantly.
"Getting laid lately?" I ask.
"All the time, but don't tell anybody," he says with his index finger to his lips.
"Women sometimes do love the crazies," I say putting my satchel down next to his bed, pulling out my laptop and Moleskin.
He looks over at me:
"You want to find out why they love the crazies?"

"Yeah," I flip open my pad, "lay it on me so I can finally get some."

He zips open his tracksuit top.

"Cause women are crazy, and crazy likes crazier," he chuckles as he licks his finger to turn the page, "makes the crazy feel sane."

"Should I write that down?"

"I'd have to charge you then," he says.

"Does your theory explain why that crazy grandma in Kiev liked you so much?"

I look down to review my notes, he asks:

"Which crazy grandma in Kiev?"

I look up and he flashes the current edition of *Carnegie Mellon Today* to show me an article, titled *Not Your Granny's Trojans,* with this description underneath: "Special: hackers now using Trojan horse hacks, using 'infinity theory,' to use in malicious software."

I shoo him away, and ask:

"There was more than one crazy grandma in Kiev?"

"You'll have to pay for that info," he says as he reads the article.

"Well," I say, "it says here in your diary there was at least one, the one in your diary where you mention about . . ."

"Yeah, her," he smirks without looking at me.

"Right, her," I nod with my pen ready to take notes.

"Yeah, yeah," he licks his left index finger, "so they sent me to Kiev to whack this Joey So-So guy."

"And when was that?"

"You know when it was," he nods over to me, "cause you got all of the numbers right there," he says

"Ok, Wilson, so they send you to Kiev, and?"

He turns the magazine vertical to stare at the centerfold, and I wonder if he is hiding something behind it.

"Hold that thought, doc, got to hit up my office real quick."

As Wilson gets up and walks past me over to the toilet, I peer down at my laptop to his Kiev diary entries. When the door to the bathroom closes, I start to read this:

<u>November 24, 2014</u>

Found out today from Still that I'm going to Kiev! Hot chicks, best vodka, and trance clubs, holy shit! This is why I joined CIA.

I don't care that he ruined my buzz about the trip with his bullshit about me needing "to get rid of him."

"The boogey man under your son's bed?" I remember saying.

I loved fucking with him.

"No, you asshole," Unger shook his swollen looking wrestler fist at me. "I need you to get rid of Ivan Borodin's guy in Kiev."

No way, I thought, Borodin had a guy? Impossible. I shrugged.

"Here's a picture of his guy, name is Joseph Sailing, otherwise known as 'Joey,' and also known as 'So-So.'"

"Whose toes did So-So step on?" I asked.

It didn't really matter. The next thing I know, I'm scheduling a plane ride to Kiev, where I am to meet my Russian contact there, Ilia.

<u>February 14, 2014</u>

"Yankee, Yankee, you come to the cold, you like the cold, eh?" Ilia said when I saw him today after he picked me up from the airport. I often called him by his code name, "MC," for "Model Citizen." His teeth reeked of vodka like he had been sleeping peacefully in a Brooklyn jail all night while his soldiers did solid dirt.

"Those waters are cold in Brighton," he said as he took one of my bags, "during the winter," he slapped my back as we walked to his shitty Chevy Nova, "so this cold must not surprise to you, da?"

He took a whiff of my black Pendleton wool shirt that was hidden underneath my tailored black bear skin coat.

"You sleep with Cheeks or Chong last night?" The tall lien figure skater looking Ilia asked me.

He slapped me on my shoulder as we sped off in his Nova.

He knew me well.

Right when I got off any plane, I always rolled one. It calmed me to sedate my nerves so I wouldn't think about where I was going, and what I was doing, to potentially feed what I liked to call the terrorism racket. Like any racket, it's acting like you are dealing with a problem to the public when you are actually milking it and keeping it alive under the table, to get a bigger budget, for example. I didn't have these doubts right after joining CIA after 9/11, but they have grown like weeds since then. I was excited to travel — scared of why I was traveling.

"I fucked Cheech and blew Chong last night, and then they gave me this joint instead of cash," I said to Ilia

"Da," he looked me up and down, "is obvious they get the shitty deal," he said deadpan.

"Want to smoke some?" I asked holding out the magnificently rolled joint.

"A little later," he pushed my hand away. "Let's have some vodka first," he said as he handed me a fancy Tiffany's flask that had some other man's initials on it, probably lifted from someone's pocket on Madison Avenue, his past time during his weekends off in New York City.

We crawled into Ilia's Nova and "sped off" to this shitty little bar on the outskirts of Kiev. Nobody was around outside except for a fire hydrant stout grandmother selling crosses on the corner, and a black cat who was spinning around her left ankle.

"Know how to pick the hot classy spots, eh?" I said over to Ilia, a stealthy double agent who took money from both U.S. and Russian clients, a sort of Hans Solo smuggler in the intelligence community. Quite a smart play, actually, since his intelligence is the best in the marketplace, but also the most expensive to cozy up to.

We walked into a dodgy BBQ bar called Joey's! Ilia told me it was a hot club – but it was a fucking dump! I thought maybe they were going to try and kill me.

Suddenly, a white haired man wearing a black wool sailor beanie said over to us through his thick Wild West looking mustache:

"Eh, come, come, Ilia, how you?" The man came over to warmly hug and kiss Ilia on the cheeks as Siberian hunters would after months of isolation.

"So-So," Ilia said to the stout man, who was the man I was sent to kill, "how you been?"

"Eh, what can I say, so-so," So-So said with a wry smile.

They giggled as boy scouts would seeing a naked woman the first time.

"Business could be better," So-So looked around the bar which was full of old men sleeping on the tables, and even another grandma who was passed out in the corner, her panties and stockings put on the table, like she had been staying there for months. Her make up kit, toothbrush, and suitcase were spread all over, too.

"And who is this Yankee?" So-So said over to me, little pieces of fish in his white mustache, showing his white gold teeth in the front of his mouth. He slapped me on the shoulder with his old wrinkled hand, and I was sort of like, yuck dirty old man. His skin color was white toilet paper that had been sitting on the floor of piss and dirty water for years – then South of France sun kissed.

"This is Dodgy, Dodgy Bond is his name," Ilia said to So-So.

"Dodgy Bond," a sort of stoner-beached boy James Bond, is one of my spy craft names, for all of you hackers that are reading my entries. I put out my hand towards the short and fit ocean diver looking old man.

"A pleasure, sir, I've been told a lot about you," I said to his beady black eyes, which looked me up and down, not sure if he was going to kill me or cook me dinner that night, cigars and brandy after.

"Any friend of Ilia is my friend," he shook my hand and looked over my shoulder. I looked behind me and a bearded bearish man yelled:

"Eh, eh, So-So, get me more vodka, get me more vodka!"

The bearded bearish man's girlfriend next to him, who basically was like a burly beardless version of him, said "dah, dah, more." She held up her short shot glass.

"Yuri," So-So yelled back, "you have enough. Stop being the shitty pants boy."

So-So then slapped my shoulder again, "come, we have the drink, da?"

We sat at a table full of gambling tools – cards, chips, & cigars. He poured me some Beluga vodka, one of my favorites.

"You drink the vodka but how about drink-

ing the soup?" So-So interrupted my thoughts as I drank the Siberian vodka.

"Please," I nodded.

He quickly got up and I pulled up my satchel full of notebooks, weed, a flask of scotch whiskey, and a cyanide tablet that I always kept with me.

"I told you he cool," Ilia said to So-So as he looked over to me. I stuck out like a malnourished American stoner among well-fed Russian wolves.

But my black bear coat kept them wondering: what would he pull out of his ass? Word in underground circles was that I had won it from a finely dressed mustached Georgian man who I pulled a Bobby Fishy on during a chess game at a Lower East Side bar.

"Here dude, have some," I handed Ilia the joint that I had rolled, and which was in my ratty Pendleton black wool board shirt.

He looked around to make sure the coast was clear, and rubbed his elegant piano player looking hands on his figure skater type tall lean torso.

"Right on, right on," he pulled the joint up to his mouth.

Ilia kept puffing cause I could tell he hadn't had any in a while in between his Beluga caviars, Beluga vodkas, and freezing nights of hot kinky apartment sex. As I stared at his long finely trimmed wizard nails I think he used to play guitar, I escaped into my memory of producing the freshest house parties with Sash on the coldest of winter nights in Brighton Beach.

"Shit, what you thinking about," Ilia said to me as he blew some smoke out of his mouth into my face.

"About a friend of mine and how we used to love Tijuana."

February 17, 2014

Far out. Woke up today at Joey's! That grandma's stockings were wrapped around my neck like a scarf, or like I was about to be choked. In the other room, I could hear that granny from last night singing as Joey made steak and eggs. I also heard Ilia spit out his coffee as he cracked up with laughter, slapping his knee: "a coup in Mexico? What bullshit!"

I thought to myself: Did I do it with her? Did she do it with me? Or did I do myself? I looked over and saw a chessboard, smoked cigars, and several ripped pieces of paper showing scores. I knew I was in big trouble, cause let's just say I wasn't supposed to be playing chess all night long. I was supposed to whack So-So.

Holy shit I was sure in big trouble!

Suddenly, Wilson comes out of his hospital room bathroom and asks:

"Think I'll make it into *Penthouse Letters* with my diaries about Kiev, doc?"

"Less men, more women, and maybe you got a shot, son," I say.

He comes over to the bed and pulls up track suit pants:

"I bet there's at least two women in there, what you talking about?"

He displays an imperceptible smirk as he picks up his Carnegie alumni magazine.

"So you overheard Ilia laughing about the Mexico coup business, and you told Director Still?" I ask.

Agent Wilson nods in the affirmative as he opens up the magazine vertically again, and focuses intently on the centerfold on the other side of the page.

"And Still took it seriously?"

Wilson nods affirmatively again as he flips the page, flashing the article to me, titled "*Digital Anonymity: Costs, Benefits*," like I would care. As he reviews the piece, he says with a miniscule smirk:

"They even started doing hearings in the House Permanent Selection Committee on Intelligence on the 'Mexico coup.'"

"But Director Still was nonetheless pissed even though you gave him the Mexican coup scoop?"

"Yeah, cause that didn't make up for me not killing So-So, even though I gave all of those lawyers in D.C. like years more work with my report about the Mexican coup, which fueled rumors President Seagull married President Puritan in a secret Las Vegas gay wedding ceremony so that Puritan would help Seagull win the 2016 election."

I write down in my Moleskin: "Mexico coup – real or red herring? Las Vegas party wedding – sounds fun."

I look back at Wilson, who looks like he couldn't be bothered.?

Sitting there next to Wilson, I stare at him obliviously looking at the Carnegie Mellon Today alumni magazine. As I do, I remember back to the day when Knox Wilson came in with those magazines. I peer back at my computer. I scroll through the e-mails surrounding the deepfake hack of those Coney Boys at Brooklyn College, and I wonder:

RUSSIAN HACKER:
"I PICK 2016 ELECTION WINNER,
LIKE MY NOSE WHEN I'M STUCK IN HORSEY TRAFFIC."

I stare at Wilson obliviously looking at the *Carnegie Mellon Today* alumni magazine. As I do, I remember back to the day when Knox Wilson came in with those magazines. I peer back at my computer. I scroll through the e-mails surrounding the bestiality hack of those Coney Boys at Brooklyn College, and I wonder:

What if the "Bill Bakes" carbon copied on the e-mails isn't Sasha or Skip's alias, as the New York City police department thought, but was Knox Wilson's, as my intuition started telling me?

I look at the time on my computer.

"Time's up," I say to Wilson.

"Got a date, old sport?" He asks.

"Yeah, with one of the Kiev grandmothers."

"Wear a condom," he says as I walk out the room.

"I'll see you in a week, Wilson," I say back with a guarded smile.

If New York's finest could have been wrong about the Bill Bakes alias, and the press's coverage of Crimea was so one-sided, then maybe the narrative marketed by President Rock Drama and others about the Russians hacking the 2016 election in collusion with President Seagull wasn't on such firm foundation, either?

I go back into my office. I close the door. I listen to a recording of Russian President Ivan Puritan attached to one of Sasha's e-mails to agent Wilson.

I had a feeling I'd soon understand things better.

/Chapter 8

DEEPFAKE LEAKS!//

The phone recording of President Borodin speaking to his Foreign Minister Yuri Arensky is scratchy, but I could hear it even over what sounds like Borodin cutting his toenails in the background:

> *Ivan: Da, da, I ordered the hack of these dumb Americans! It is the, how they say, so the much easy. Like be the Scottish man with the kilt have the sexy times with the sheep, nyet?*

> *Crack, goes a cut toenail in the background.*

> *Sassy: It is the too funny. Who the fuck needs Randy Murphy to laugh?*

> *Crack, goes another cut toenail in the background.*

> *Ivan: Nyet, Eddie Murphy.*

> *Sassy: Da, him, the architect.*

The recording is affixed to an e-mail from Sasha to Skip, dated July 4, 2016, that is copied to "Steve Robs," who I hadn't heard of before, with this message:

> *This should do the trick.*

Wondering who this "Steve Robs" was, and suspecting it was another false flag alter ago name for Sasha or Skip but wondering if it was Knox, my thoughts were suddenly interrupted by my memory of what Wilson said to me once about his view of the 2016 Russians hacking of the Democratic National Committee documents, not long after he was first admitted.

He said something like:

"Doc, if the hacking code walks like a Russian, smells like a Russian, and talks like a Russian, then I can tell you it's a probably a shitty wicked smart assed basement dwelling American who, unbeknownst to the CIA, is one of their contractors."

Suddenly, I hear the Otis the janitor's thick English accent through my office door:

"Finished with today's rubbish, Doctor Egan?"

"Yeah, Otis, come on in."

The regally tall janitor with white hair down to his shoulders comes in, with filthy hands and nails, smiling at me through his dirty face.

"Why are you working this late, old chap?" He asks. "I don't' believe you get bonuses."

"Yeah, but I got some extra stuff to do here," I say staring at my computer. I could see him from the corner of my eye slyly peaking at my computer screen as he smirked.

"Oh, please, there's much more privacy yat your abode, is there not?"

I look over at him and smirk. He chuckles as he throws the garbage into his larger hamper, concentrating through his pricey looking little Benjamin Franklin glasses. I always thought it mysterious how this janitor could afford those on his salary. He then says to me:

"Mother used to say that humor is the apple to cure our mental pettiness."

"Certainly," I say like a parrot, not paying too much attention to what he just said cause I was so in the weeds of what I was reading.

He starts walking out my office.

"Good night, Otis," I say.

"Good evening, good doctor."

He slowly closes the door.

As he does, his word, "npettiness," insidiously echoes in my head. I suddenly giggle, remembering that Napoleon Bonaparte, the actual inventor of the "blitzkrieg" (it wasn't Adolf the Austrian), was a sneaky man like this janitor Otis. But most of the French bourgeoisie "establishment" discounted Napoleon because their nationalistic "pettiness" made them blind to his genius all because he was Corsican born.

Similarly, I tend to discount what agent Wilson had been telling me because of the hype running around my head by the likes of establishment figures in the CIA, and the constant contrary barrage of reports from the American press about still yet evidenced "Russian hacking" that miraculously caused President Seagull to win the election. I then ask myself out loud:

Could agent Wilson be telling the truth?

My phone alarm goes off. I need to head home to feed my black fish, Alberto. As I start to leave, I figure I'd come back to this issue sometime soon. On my way home, driving in my midnight blue Saturn SL2 to Oyster Bay, I couldn't get what agent Wilson said to me about the rumored Russian hacking out of my head.

So, when I get home, I open up an imperial stout and go online. As Alberto stares at me wondering if he was ever going to get laid again, I drink some of the Rasputin pint as I open up a *New York Times* article I saved from the summer of 2016:

WIKI LEAKS:
HACKED DNC E-MAILS—GET THEM HERE!

The date of the article is July 22, 2016. I flip to some of the other pieces I had saved, and find another one, dated December 9, 2016, Washington Post article:

RRUSSIANS HACKED 2016 ELECTION
AMBASSADORS OUSTED

According to the article, proof for the conclusion was in various sources, including in "classified reports" by private outfits . I have access to one classified report, dated December 28, 2016, which reads:

> *Same code, same actor, blah, blah – we've totally seen this code only from Russian linked sources in the Ukraine when they hacked cell phones over there, so you can think of it as smelly vodka drenched fingerprints left on your girlfriend's tits—or boyfriend's cock, if you roll that way.*

But I have other articles in the file, like in this interview of Mr. Ron McDonald, who founded McDonald LLC security and sold it for $7.18 billion in 2010 to Intel, in Wired magazine:

> *It's a fact that hackers have the ability to get into your system using Trojan horses that may have several identities over their true one in order to hack anonymously, kind of like how a small cock can be made to look huge with twenty rubbers on it, not that I'd know.*

Still browsing another article, this one about the massive leak of CIA snooping technology earlier this year, on March 7, 2017, I saw that everything that Mr. McDonald said was correct, even though some poo-poo him in the mainstream because of his eccentricities:

> *Raw Deal, a CIA program that allows you to search surreptitiously in someone's computer without anyone knowing you are in the person's computer system or, when you are caught, making it look like someone else, say the Russians! Think of living out your dirtiest fantasies through an alter ego, and blaming it all on someone else when you get caught. That's Raw Deal!*

Curious, I do a search for the youngest hackers. I pull up a list of teenage hackers, some as young as 13, who have "hacked everything." All of the hackers on the list are American.

So, I had to wonder, how could all of President Drama's intelligence experts conclude with "high confidence," or with any confidence for that matter, that the Russians hacked the 2016 election? The more I thought about it, the more I questioned the truth of comments like this from Assistant Director Cross in a May 23, 2017, *Washington Post* article, which I pull up on my computer:

> *With Hercules like confidence, we can conclude that it was the Russians, and that President Puritan personally directed it. I mean, in intelligence gathering, you are never going to be certain, but this rating on the quality of the intelligence gives it credibility to act on, kind of like when you know a woman is a woman, not a transvestite, by looking at her, you know?*

When I read Assistant Director Cross's statement, the AAA credit ratings of those garbage mortgage backed securities investments that led to the 2008 financial crash march into my head.

Suddenly, there is a loud knock on my door.

"Doc, your pizza, man, pizza," Jake Vivaldi says through the thick wooden doors, as my black labs dogs, Duke and Lila, wake up from their naps. I look over and catch Alberto looking at the dogs, staring at Lila like they maybe will make out one day. Like father, like fish.

"Yeah, yeah, coming," I say.

Jake runs an organic vegan fair trade co-op farm, called *Vino*, not far from where my little cabin is in Oyster Bay, where he also cooks up some Neapolitan pizza.

I open the door and Jake the brick shit house built pizza man smiles as he holds up a six-pack of Budweiser, a box of Italian cigars, and a box of homemade Italian sausage pizza.

"Fuck yeah," I give his construction worker tough but manicured hand a high five. "If you were just a little better looking, I'd kiss you."

"Yeah, yeah, even with a new six pack," he looks at his tummy, "I couldn't do anything for that," he looks down between my legs with a hopeless face.

"And thank goodness for that, thank goodness," I join him looking at my crotch.

Duke and Lila come up and sniff him.

"Eh, someone likes sniffing me," he pats the dogs on their heads.

"Better them than me," his wife Nina Vivaldi says walking up the driveway, a former model from Ghana and part-time lecturer at the University of Sorbonne in Paris, following in her mother and grandmother's good steps. She looks down at the dogs.

Jake looks up at me, smiles, and says:

"See why I keep her around?"

I kiss Nina on both cheeks. She hands me a bottle of pinot noir from Oregon, one of my favorites. We all walk into the kitchen and stand around the island, where I was preparing a red kale salad for dinner, and had setup a cheese plate for munchies time, before they came. A small blue hookah is on the shelf behind me, a gift from one of my patients. I bring it out.

"Gin or vodka?" I ask Nina for her martini.

"Vodka, you know that," she smiles, her hand pointing at me from her fashion tight overalls that wrap around her breasts perfectly, "you know what gin does to me."

She then plays with Duke and Lila.

"Coming right up." I start to make her drink.

Jake goes over to the stereo and puts on *Van Morrison Live at the Hollywood Bowl*, one of my favorites. He starts doing his Italian man overbite, worse than the white man overbite. That's because Jake's slick black American-Apparel t-shirt, fitted black Levi's 501 jeans, and black and white Converse Weapon basketball sneakers give you the impression he might actually be able to dance.

"Here," I hand a fancy martini glass over to Nina. She takes it in her long elegant hand, sipping as she slips off her tomato red espadrilles, kicking them over to the front of the door, where Jake had already taken off his Weapons.

"Merci, cherie," she says to me with a small pleased smile.

"Yeah, you know how to make mine, partner," Jake's mouth says through a Wild West looking black mustache that would make Joseph Stalin jealous in an *American Psycho* business card type of way. Jake's eyes peer at me eagerly through his fancy grey and white tortoise framed eyes glasses.

I mix up Jake's Old Fashioned drink, using a secret recipe passed down from pappy Egan, the rumored Boston smuggler I told you about earlier. As I do, I think back to how my pop's pitch white Irish skin contrasted with his rainy day County Cork coast demeanor, unless he was telling a joke.

And then he'd make you piss your pants – or skinny panties.

"Tip me later, pal," I say to Jake as I hand him the drink, his chunky retired boxer hand wrapping itself all over the wet glass as he walks into my office to drop off the cigars, which I smoke here and there.

I sip my own martini.

"What you doing over here, doing some digging into ancient history?" Jake asks as he looks at my open computer screen with all of the newspaper articles about the 2016 "hack," "leak," "fix," of the "election."

"Not that ancient," I say.

"More ancient than today's spot price of oil, see that shit go way up?" He walks back over into the kitchen and looks over at me, showing the skills that got him a job counseling Blue Water Equities, Inc., a private equity firm, on financial markets. Didn't want to get into too deep with Jake about what I was doing at the hospital, it being confidential and all, but I trusted him enough to give him this:

"Got a patient who says someone in the CIA, or a CIA contractor, hacked the DNC in 2016," I shrug mixing the red kale salad, putting in some fresh garlic, and then sipping my filthy martini. I drop the things, walk into my office, and grab some photos. I hand Jake some of the supposedly hacked e-mails and deep fake photos of from a farm in Woodstock, New York, that were given to Wiki Leaks. They look real – but they were deep fakes.

"Whoa!" Jake shrugs as he sips his Old Fashioned, "Who needs to drop acid when you got them shots?"

He looks over at me

Nina shook her head.

"What is this asshole drinking?" She says looking over at me.

We all giggle. I take a long hit of the hookah. It calms my nerves a little. I get into the Zen of salad making.

"But, seriously," Jake says coming over closer to me, tapping me on the shoulder, "who is this patient of yours, and what's he really saying?"

Jake plays with the straw in his drink, puts it into a small puzzle, like he is getting some new fascinating intelligence on a whole new financial market.

I shrug. He smiles, listens, watching Nina play tug of war with the dogs.

"My patient says that this whole thing with the Russians hacking the DNC and producing deepfake photos during the 2016 was just a bunch smoke and mirrors, that it was some basement dwelling American that was a CIA contractor, whether they knew it or not I don't know."

"Yeah, yeah," Jake waves me off, "that's why he is your patient."

"Maybe, maybe," I start to stir Jake's next drink cause I know he'll be asking soon, "but he makes some interesting points that I hadn't thought of before, like how hackers online can disguise themselves so much so that you can keep chasing their fake identities forever, with new ones being created every time you think you found your culprit."

Jake looks at me, shrugging. He smiles as he takes the newly made old fashioned that I made for him and raises it to give me a cheers.

"What you say got me thinking about Chicago," he slowly sips his drink, "how some white bank robbers that ran with a guy named Blue used to put black face on when they did their business in the 1800s, got all the feds thinking it black not white men who did the dirt."

Stirring the red kale salad, with Nina playing with the dogs, and Jake "dancing" to Van Morrison, I go back into my home office and pull up the e-mails from Sasha and Skip about the *Me So Boring* software. All of the e-mails are copied to "Bill Bakes." I start pulling up the e-mails surrounding the hack of those Coney Boys at Brooklyn College, and confirm they were also copied to "Bill Bakes." I then pull up the e-mail with President Ivan Borodin's deep fake recording attached it to it, and start to stare at the carbon copy to "Steve Robs," with the Google e-mail address being srobs@gmail.com.

"Boring," I say out loud, scratching my head, and thinking back to the first time I met Knox Wilson, his shy demeanor, and his low-key way of being that contrasted with his brother's "dirty beach boy" personality.

"Could Bill Bakes and Steve Robs be Knox Wilson?" I wonder to myself. "Could Knox be the basement dwelling American hacker of the 2016 election?"

I think of *Pretty in Pink* faced Knox Wilson. I then look back at the e-mail that supposedly attached these recordings of Puritan and Sassy, reflecting on Jake's Chicago story of at least some white men under the direction of this Blue character camouflaged as black men robbing banks in the 1800s.

Thinking back to agent Wilson's artificial intelligence foreign language earpiece from Afghanistan, I sit there picturing Knox in his Brooklyn basement with his girlfriend with the raspberry colored beret. He invents the code and technology for his brother's earpiece, and also for the voice over technology. I imagine Knox and his girlfriend giggling together as they record the conversions between Puritan and Sassy, and play gunslinger with their fingers or toy pirate guns.

After all, Knox certainly had the motive for the hacks on those Coney Boys because they picked on him. He also had the motive to plant the deepfake photos on DNC's computers and e-mails because, as I understand things, some made fun of "basement dwellers." I then I remember that "Basement Dwellers Inc." pin affixed to Knox's messenger bag with the kids' hands above pulling the strings when he came into his brother's room. I didn't get the impression he cared about politics, this Knox. But I also do think he cares about not being spit on with words by anyone merely because he lives in his parents' basement.

My phone buzzes in my shirt pocket. I pick it up. A text message from Director Still reads:

Dr. Egan, let's get Wilson tried.

I put the phone down, waving it off, and thought to check whether the IP addresses for both "Bill Bakes" and "Steve Robs" e-mail addresses were the same. I go to the website whatismyipaddress.com, and plug in the information for both of the e-mails.

I couldn't believe my eyes.

/Chapter 9:

∧BASEMENT DWELLERS, INC+

"**H**oly shit," I say to myself, "they are the same." The IP address for "Bill Bakes" and "Steve Robs" is: 173.196.49.198.

I sit back in my chair. I picture this Knox Wilson sitting in his Brighton Beach basement with his girlfriend sitting next to him as he creates thousands of e-mail addresses, each with different IP addresses or sometimes sharing the same one, like these two for "Bill Bakes" and "Steve Robs."

"Holy shit," I say again as I leave my home office and party the rest of the evening with Jake and Nina, then crash.

Two days later, in the early morning of November 9, 2017, I hear someone yelling from the hospital waiting room, "it's starting, starting, it's starting!"

Wondering what the hell is going on, and also needing a break, I put my computer into sleep mode and walk over to the waiting room, where I find an elegant looking finely mustached man with an iv hanging out of his arm yelling at the television with a tinge of an accent, "where is *Top Gun*, I want my *Top Gun*! What the fuck is this?" I look up and see President Seagull on NBC news announcing:

*Ladies and gentlemen, we are getting ready
to launch cruise missiles towards Tijuana to take
out those Russian missiles.*

Fed up, the lean mustached man with circular spectacles standing next to me switches the channel to CBS, which had Mr. Pepper with a pie chart.

Sitting there watching the continuity of colors on the chart, how they were all connected even though they each occupied their own silo of color on the chart, I think to myself: if this basement dweller Knox could have used two e-mail addresses like that for one IP address, and sent or received e-mails like they were different people, what other e-mails have I received were from a camouflaged Knox Wilson?

"Have a good morning, mister?" I lean over, hold out my hand, and say to the maybe not so retired composer looking man with my hand out. "I'm Doctor Egan."

"Da, da, friends call me Fyodor," he says with a grin as he shakes my hand.

He winks at me in a "we are on the same team type of way," and I wonder if he is gay.

I get nervous. I slowly pull my hand out of his. I walk away. I hear him turn the channel back to NBC and *Top Gun* blares in the background as he cheers, "da, da, go Tom, get her back, don't be such the gutless pretty boy."

As I walk back to my office, I wonder: haven't I seen that thinly mustached man somewhere before?

After I get back into my office, I finish the red kale salad, and open my computer back up to Wilson's file. There is a list of e-mails on the right hand side of my screen, the most recent one from Director Stan Still at the top.

I open the e-mail up, and look at the domain. It's: dstill@cia.gov. Just like the other ones I received. Curious, I do a search online for e-mail scamming, wondering if there was some way this Knox Egan could have somehow sent e-mails using Director Still's e-mail account. I discover that there is a way to change the headers of e-mails so that they trick your e-mail system into thinking they are from Director Still when, in fact, they are from an imposter like Knox Wilson. Think of it like you would someone who picks the lock of your house, or uses disguises themselves as a "VIP" to sneak into a hot New York City nightclub.

Clicking on the header of Director Still's recent e-mail, I cut and paste it into a find an e-mail source website online.

I discover the e-mail I opened up from Director Still has the same IP address as the CIA: 192.251.226.206.

Then I click on an older e-mail from Director Still, this one dated September 26, 2017, and it says:

A dirty, filthy, untrustworthy Russian has raped Wilson's mind. He used their friendship from Brooklyn as a way to crowbar his way into Wilson's psyche.

I cut and paste the e-mail header of the e-mail above into the same website.

"No way," I say out loud as I discover that the IP address for the September 26, 2017, e-mail is the same for the "Steve Robs" and "Bill Bakes" e-mail addresses, namely srobs@gmail.com and bbakes@gmail.com. Then I wonder: how many of these Unger e-mails are from this IP address, which I suspect is the basement dweller IP address in Brooklyn for that twerp Knox, and how many are from the real Director Unger?

"Deep fake," I say to myself, "deep fake," I say to myself again, remembering back to the photos planted on those Brooklyn College boys' computers and on DNC's servers.

Then I whisper " deep fake boomerang" as I sit staring as the little leaves of red kale salad left in my Tupperware bowl, wondering: how much false flag intelligence was planted by Knox and which would boomerang if relied on in this Tijuana missile crisis?

Deeply worried that this whole crisis is a case of mistaken identity, like when you are with a call girl only to discover she is a tranny when you are in the middle of performing the contract, I go to check in on agent Wilson. I desperately want to ask him some questions about his brother Knox.

Goosebumps cover my skin when I arrive into Wilson's room around 11:37 on the morning of November 9, 2017.

/CHAPTER 10:

"=ORIGINAL GENTLEMEN}

"Holy fucking shit," I say to myself when I get into Wilson's room and turn on the lights.

He isn't in his bed.

He isn't in the bathroom.

I pick up the phone. I report that Wilson has gone missing. I think to myself that he'd surely show up on one of the cameras. That's when I look down and see a small shadow underneath his nightstand. After I hang up the phone, I bend down, and I see a small compartment that was affixed with a magnet to the bottom of the metal nightstand.

"What do we have here," I say as I pick up the secret compartment, a larger version of the one that you would store an extra key in.

I open it up.

About two dozen or so ripped pieces of paper pop out of the compartment. They drip all over the ground, along with a small pencil. I pick up a piece of paper. Written in pencil on the paper:

"Super kinky athletic—Viking volleyball hot– 415.343.6877."

I pick up another:

"Epic imagination—dirty French – 202.745.7654."

Suddenly, images of the Nordic looking volleyball player tall nurse and the country French nurse with freckles that I saw in the hospital hallway pop into my head. I always wondered why there were so many different nurses tending to agent Wilson, and why they were all stunning lookers.

This little compartment gives me the answer.

The phone suddenly rings.

I pick it up.

It's hospital security: "there's no recording of agent Wilson leaving that room, Dr. Egan. No recording at all. Just nurses going in and out of his room."

I hang up the phone.

In a panic, I call Dr. Rick Rubin, President Seagull's chief doctor.

"Rick," I say when he answers his cell.

"That's me," Rick says.

"I got to ask you to check into something," I say.

"You are a brunette, Liam, not a blond, accept it," he says as I could hear him eat what I pictured was a red kale salad in the background.

He got me into being a foodie during our days at Harvard Medical School.

"Yeah, yeah," I say in response to his dark humor, "but maybe those hot rods aren't being used to build missiles in Tijuana."

"Come again?" I hear him shove some of the salad into his mouth.

"Get one of your handful of oddball CIA or FBI agents to check this company out," I tell him the name of the distribution company in Tijuana, Einstein Trucking. "See if they had any shipments around the time they told you that missiles were discovered of either raw chocolate shipments, or airplane part shipments."

There is silence on the phone.

"You are fucking joking dude, right?" He finally says. "Are you sure you aren't seeing things with all of the stress you've been under to get this Wilson guy?"

"Yeah, well, he's gone," I say, looking around Wilson's room. "Maybe he's not as nuts as everybody thinks he is."

"What the fuck!" Rick says. "Gone?"

"Gone," I say again looking down at the mouthpiece on my cell phone, "he has disappeared."

There is more silence on the phone.

"I don't get it, what do you mean he's gone?" Rick says.

"I mean what I say." I sit down on Wilson's bed, browsing at all of the *Carnegie Mellon Today* magazines on the metal nightstand. "Just please do as I ask, it won't take long to check into this."

There is silence on the phone as he thinks.

During the silence, I pick up one of the *Carnegie Mellon Today* magazines, start flipping through it, and see that a few of the centerfold type spreads that I thought were about science were, in fact, of *Playboy* models that were glued in.

I shake my head.

"Please, Rick," I say this time with more urgency, "let's be careful. This guy isn't crazy like Director Unger and Assistant Director Madison think," I cover my eyes with my hand.

"Alright, alright," he finally says as I could hear him wiping his face. "I'll get someone here to check into it."

"Someone you trust, who won't leak this to *The New York Times* or *The Washington Post*, and who won't use regular channels that leakers use," I say.

"Roger," Rick says, "my homos are super tight."

We hang up the phone.

From about 11:30 a.m. that November 9th morning to 12:30 p.m., I peek through some more of the *Carnegie Mellon Today* magazines, and find that some of the other centerfolds in the older editions are blueprints for larger passenger planes, whereas other plans are labeled *"Industrial Chocolate – Do's and Don'ts!"*

I sit there suspecting that Knox Wilson had quietly given his brother all of this intelligence right under my nose, and thought of how it would somehow be used to backfire if World War III was started because of the fake news surrounding "Tijuana missile crisis."

Frustrated that a person like agent Wilson who should have been considered a patriot was treated by some as an enemy, eI slowly walk to my office, wondering if everything in agent Wilson's file at CIA was as it appeared.

Was I missing something?

After I get back into my office, I do some research online about hacks of the CIA, and get a bunch of articles by *The New York Times*, *The Wall Street Journal*, and others about the huge one that happened right after agent Wilson applied to CIA on November 6, 2001. According to one article from *The New York Times* on November 8, 2001:

> *Home addresses, family information, and even very personal birthmark information of people like Director Unger and Assistant Director Madison was either released, or potentially tampered with. Agent files suspected modified.*

So this infiltration of the CIA on November 7, 2001 could have modified Wilson's application, hiding something that not even Director Unger or Assistant Director Madison knew about him.

Suddenly, I get a text message from Rick.

It's now about 1:00 p.m. on November 9, 2017:

> *Turns out there were some shipments of chocolate rods by Einstein Trucking to a plant in Tijuana, partially owned by Skinny Carlo under another name, I think the last name was Sanchez, otherwise he wouldn't be "skinny," right?*

> *Anyway, President Hess has been made aware of*

these shipments and the benign alternative explanation for what our AI in the satellite saw, and has been in touch with President Borodin.

We just avoided World War III!

And it's because of your "crazy" agent.

Maybe he went to Disneyland to party? Or maybe he went to his silent partner's brothel in Amsterdam for free massages?

Martinis soon?

"Holy Jesus mother Mary of Christ," I did a sign on my chest of the Father, the Son, the Holy Spirit, even though I hadn't been to church with anybody else since my parents took me once to reschedule my baptism. That's a pretty long time, right? I lay back in my chair, closing my eyes to rest for a few minutes. It's about 3:00 p.m. in the morning on Thursday, November 9, and I know I need some shuteye or else I'm going to faint.

So I head out of the hospital, head home, and sleep for almost the whole weekend.

When Monday, November 13, 2017, comes around, I still have this nagging curiosity about where agent Wilson went, if that's his real name. So I make a phone call to a New York City attorney family friend, named Melvin "Mel" Hyman, Esq., whose family of lawyers have been representing my family since at least the 1800s, maybe before.

"I got someone for you to check out," I say to Mel when he picks up.

"What's her name?" He responds.

"Come on, I'm being serious."

"Hey, me too, you think I'm a dead man who can't look at no broads no more?"

"It's a man, his name is Skip Wilson, and he's an agent in CIA."

"Sounds like fun, what he'd do, pole dancing?"

"I think he or his brother have been hacking into CIA e-mails for some time now. They might have been working with this Russian Sasha Stravinska character, too, who I'd like you to check out after you get the info on Skip."

"Why wouldn't he do that hacking into *Playboy*? Dummy." I hear Mel write. He asks: "Got this Wilson's social security number, birthday, license or passport?"

I shuffle through Wilson's file, pick out his social security number, read it to Mel:

"696-69-6969."

"Sounds fishy," Mel says as he writes, "cause I never heard one like that before. Send me the rest of the info to my secretary, and I'll get my guy on it."

"Regular rate?" I ask.

The regular rate is that Mel would barter his time for mine, which he needed sometimes to independently judge experts he hired for criminal trials. Not all experts are the same. Some will say whatever you want, even when what you have to say doesn't make any sense, to make the buck.

"Yeah, doc," regular rate, "I'll get my guy on this, and should be back to you in a week or so."

"Thank you, you are a pal."

"Yeah, whatever, just keep sending business my way."

We hang up the phone. About a week later, on November 20, 2017, I'm sitting back in my office when I get this call from Mel:

"You won't believe this shit, doc," Mel says.

"You reversed your sex change?" I ask.

"Nah, too expensive. Plus, I get away with a lot more bullshit being a miniature ballbuster than some pushy New York JAP broad. Anyway, I got better for you."

"Hit me with it," I play with my coffee cup.

"Yeah, so turns out this agent you been treating, Skip Wilson, he is from Brighton Beach like he said."

"Yeah?" I ask.

"Yeah."

"And what about his brother, his family?" I ask.

"They all from Brighton, like he said."

"Okay, okay, good news," I say.

"And I had my guys check out this Sasha character, too, on the house, and everything checks out. His records from Brooklyn Tech, his name, all of it," Mel says.

"So what's the big news then?" I ask.

"Well, this Skip Wilson character, that's not his real name, and that social security number you gave me from his CIA file was doctored."

I look outside the window of my office onto Brooklyn's waters.

"What's his real name?" I ask.

"Jimmy Hoffa the III," Mel says.

I look at the mouth peace of the phone.

"Come on, seriously."

"Alright, take it easy," he takes a sip of his coffee or maybe it was his afternoon scotch, "his real last name is Black"

"Black, huh?"

"Yeah, not white and I'm not being racist."

"Yeah, yeah, give me the info, I don't have all century for your malarkey."

He was silent. I could tell he was smirking quietly. Then he says:

"Skip's real first name is Knox. Full name is Knox Black."

I look up to the ceiling, wondering.

"I'll be damned. And what's his little brother's name?"

Mel shuffles some papers, and then he says:

"Brother's real first name is Winston. Full name is Winston Black II, evidently kid's named for his grandpa, who was some spook during WWII."

"Evidently, his grandpa was black?" I ask.

"No, you Harvard educated idiot, don't they teach you anything at that school? Spook is the old school slang for a spy."

I wrote down in my diary: "Spook – can use without being racist. Cool name!"

"How'd your guy find all this out?" I ask Mel.

"He's got his ways, trade secret stuff."

"Silk Road, isn't that a sexual position?" I ask.

"Huh," I could picture him shrugging, "if it isn't, it should be."

I take a long sip of my coffee. I have a small pleased smirk on my face, remembering when my pop used to tell me, "all's well that ends well."

"But you don't know where this Knox Black is now?" I ask Mel.

"No clue," he says, "I had my guy check, and he must be lying low somewhere."

"And his little brother?"

"He moved out of his parent's basement, according to his neighbors, who say he hasn't been around the neighborhood in months, say they saw a bunch of movers one day."

I lean back in my chair, satisfied that I got to the bottom of what had been a very stressful few weeks with the Tijuana missile crisis and all.

"Thanks, Mel," I finally say.

"Anytime, doc," he says taking another sip.

We hang up the phone.

A few years later, sometime in October of 2019, I'm in New York City on a long weekend, to meet a woman, Aden Gordon, who I met at a conference on the untapped powers of the subconscious mind at Stanford University. Her family runs a charity, called "Veritas," that her grandmother, Sophia Gordon, founded not long after the end of WWII. I am super excited to meet her, cause we've been e-mailing for some time, and I'm waiting for her at The Carlyle in on the Upper East Side of New York. I take out my copy of *Forbes Magazine* from my messenger bag. I browse through articles, and then get to the back, where I find a B-movie looking ad for jacuzzi bathtubs, with 1980s bikini clad women surrounding this man who looks suspiciously familiar as he stands in the middle of the bathtub flexing his slightly flabby muscles.

I take a closer look.

The bushy Jerry Garcia bearded slightly overweight man had the same eyes as Agent Knox Black (a/k/a "Skip Wilson" a/k/a "Dodgy Bond"), same smile, and, plus, I could see the outline of a birthmark on the right side of his neck, the one I noticed when I first met him. I look up to the headline for the ad, and it reads:

Superstar French actors
enjoy our Jacuzzis!
So why shouldn't you?

"It couldn't be," I say to myself, inspecting the vintage looking photo of what I think is Knox, wondering if he either put on weight or was wearing some type of extra skin suit for the shoot. I look to the right of the Jacuzzi, and there is a finely trimmed 1940's mustached "fashion" photographer directing the scene holding an old Leica camera. I look closer, at his eyes, as he waves to one of the models, who is flirting with him, and then I say to myself: "Sasha?"

"They must have known I had a subscription to *Forbes*," I say to myself under my breath, "that this was their tricky way of getting in touch."

I turn the *Forbes* magazine over, and look at the front cover.

There is large crisp photo of Skinny Carlo smoking a cigar, with some people in the background representing some of the tech companies he has funded, one of the tech company owners looks like Winston Black II (a/k/a "Knox Wilson," "Bill Bakes," "Steve Robs"), albeit with longer dread locked blonde hair with brown streaks smoking a cigar. A shabby 1980s hand-held radio is on the ground, looks like the same one that agent Black (a/k/a "Wilson") and Professor Wu listened to. When I check inside the mag to see the names of those on the front, I see a whole profile on Winston and his company, *Dirty French*, which enables "adult virtual sex across different platforms from anywhere in the world, but no bestial allowed."

I smirk to myself.

When Aden comes down, she looks glorious. I can't believe I'm with a woman like her. We talk walking towards the front door of the hotel, which I open for her.

"Such the gentleman," she says with a smirk on her face, stunning steel blue eyes glazing at me.

When I was a kid, they used to say the Devil is a gentleman.

But he's obviously not the original one.

These three quiet winners from Brighton Beach showed me that.

The End